DARK
SECRET

DARK

SECRET

DARKHAVEN SAGA: BOOK ONE

DANIELLE ROSE

WATERHOUSE PRESS

ISBN: 978-1-64263-165-4

For Aunt Michelle—
for believing in me then,
for guiding me now.
This one is for you.

ONE

The house is silent save for the howling wind outside. It threatens us with the commotion of an incoming storm—its strength and fury already enough to send the occasional tree branch crashing against my windowpanes.

This is the first time I've had to sneak out to go on patrol. The thought doesn't sit well with me. I'm used to trust and freedom, not the threat of banishment.

Tossing my covers aside, I sit up and allow my legs to dangle over the side of my bed. I'm already dressed. I began preparing for this moment as soon as *Mamá* told me I wasn't allowed to hunt tonight.

Instinctively, I reach for my necklace. I run my thumb down the length of the cross, my strength rejuvenated by its mere presence. The metal is cold to my touch. This two-inch silver cross is the last thing *Papá* gave me before he sacrificed himself to save Mamá and me from vampires. I never take it off.

I glance around my room in search of his portrait, but I don't find it. For the first time, I'm thankful Mamá is having the frame redone. I can't bear the thought of him watching—not tonight. Not until I have proof.

I tiptoe across the room, careful not to step on loose floorboards, and slip into my combat boots. I've strategically placed them in front of my dresser, which is directly to the right of my bedroom door.

I'm just feet from my escape now. My breath comes in shallow huffs, and my hands are clammy. I can't wait to feel the cool breeze against my skin. I wipe my palms against my jeans and try to shake off the fear of being discovered.

I stare at my reflection in the large mirror that hangs on the wall above my dresser and replay each scenario in my mind. Mamá will not be pleased when she discovers I've disobeyed her order to retire early and skip my patrol. But I must ignore her. I can't skip even one night of patrol in favor of rest before our upcoming full moon ritual.

For weeks now, I've been burdened by the truth. Nestled deep within the pit of my gut is the feeling that something horrible will soon befall my coven. When I told Mamá, she simply made me a potion mixed with dandelion, wormwood, and calendula herbs to aid my clairvoyance and encourage psychic development. Her disbelief stings. Being the only other spirit witch in our coven, she is supposed to trust my instincts. I may be a novice compared to her, but I still know the signs of impending doom.

Quickly, I tie my hair back and assess my look. I carefully choose my attire for every patrol. Tonight, I'm wearing all black—not unusual for me. My clothes are tight, yet loose enough to sidestep attacks. My jeans are tucked into my boots, and my long-sleeved shirt has small holes that loop around my thumbs, keeping it in place. My exposed neck is protected by my cross.

Missing only two things, I'm nearly ready to begin my patrol.

I grab the small mesh baggie. Last night, I filled it with

horehound and mugwort. They're strong herbs used in protection spells. These aren't a guarantee, but they can't hurt. And I'll take anything I can get. Usually I try to patrol with another witch, but tonight I'm going alone. It's reckless, but I don't have another choice. I must hunt until this uneasy feeling goes away.

A long, narrow black box rests atop my dresser. I open the lid. Something washes over me every time I see it, touch it. I run a finger down the long, cool metal, and a jolt of energy shoots down my spine.

What started as plain, bright, and reflective silver is now a formidable weapon. On one end, it's thick and fits firmly in my hand. On the other, it's pointed into a sharp dagger.

Forged by witches, the metal was melted into its liquid state and mixed with the strongest protection elixirs. No longer shiny, the weapon, my stake, is a matte dark gray and etched with runes that represent magic, the elements, death, and power.

When I grasp at it to pick it up, it rolls into the palm of my hand as if it somehow *knows* it should be there. It's nothing but metal and magic, but it feels alive. It feels like it's part of me, and as a spirit witch, with little control over the elements, I rely heavily on this stake. It's saved my neck more times than I care to admit.

I tighten my grasp around it, and suddenly I'm no longer afraid to sneak away and hunt vampires.

I don't fear Mamá's reaction or care what the coven thinks. All I can think about is driving this stake into a vampire's heart and ridding the world of another monster.

I slip the stake into its sheath, which hangs comfortably against my side. Hidden by my arms, blissfully unaware humans don't notice it. Of course, vampires do. Their senses are far greater than mine. Their strength and speed are unmatched. But they haven't access to the earth's magic, and that, in the end, is always the reason why they bite the dust and I make it home for dinner.

I consider staging my room so it looks like I'm sleeping. I could adjust my pillows to make them mirror the shape of my body, but I shrug away the thought. I'm only planning a quick loop around the village. I should be back long before Mamá wakes.

My door creaks as I open it, and I freeze. Seconds tick by. I poke my head past the threshold and scan the hallway. Mamá's door is still closed. I listen for her soft snoring, my racing thoughts slowing with each exhale.

I tiptoe down the hall and press my ear to her door. If she catches me, I will tell her I am just going to the bathroom. Or maybe I'll say I can't sleep, so I'm going downstairs for a snack. Of course, she'd see through both lies. Mamá is a natural lie detector. But I'd have to try.

No noise comes from her room, save for her heavy breathing. I rub my cross for strength and dash through the hall and down the stairs, skidding to a stop at the front door. Before I even realize what I'm doing, I'm grasping the doorknob, twisting, yanking, and pulling the solid oak open and then closed behind me.

The cool breeze sends a shiver down my spine. I pull my jacket tighter around me to keep out the cold night air and wipe the sweat that's beaded at my temple. Slowly, I turn to face the outside world.

Our house is still dark. Every other step, I toss a glance behind me until I'm so far down the street I can't see home anymore. There's nothing but dark space, guilt, and dread between Mamá and me now.

I don't cherish the thought of upsetting her. Some of my worst memories are from times when she's told me I've disappointed her. My very worst memory is when I was too young to help her and Papá. I was the ultimate disappointment.

I kick the pebbles at my feet. I tried explaining how important patrols are right now, but Mamá wouldn't listen. It's frustrating that she believes in my magic as a spirit witch, but she doesn't believe in *me*. Something dark is coming, I know it, and it's heading straight for our coven. If she won't protect them, I will, even if it means lying, sneaking out, keeping secrets, and breaking promises.

The streetlights are bright at this time of night, illuminating the world around me in rays of light, showcasing all the things I don't notice during the day. That's my favorite part about patrolling. Mamá doesn't understand why I love it so much—the hunting, tracking, killing. But there's something about the way the moon speaks to me. It's like she sings songs for my ears alone. She calls to me in ways Mamá doesn't understand. I am destined for the night. For the hunt.

The witches aren't very good at training me to fight. Rather than using hand-to-hand combat, they rely on their magical affinities for one of the five elements—earth, air, water, fire, and spirit. Even as a coven at full strength, the slightest hiccup can prevent a successful ritual.

Since witches are earthly vessels, our power is finicky and dependent on too many outside factors. To perform a ritual properly and to cast even a simple spell, timing matters. We're servants to the moon, to the sun, and to the seasons.

Our magic is so much a part of us, it affects witches on a

cellular and characteristic level.

A naturally masculine element, fire witches are passionate and creative, and harness a fierce temperament. Fire witches can ignite a flame within their victims, burning them alive, but the element is only at its strongest during midday on a summer afternoon.

The other masculine element is air. Air witches are wise, intellectual beings who rationalize even the most chaotic of times. They can hack through skin with forceful blasts of wind, but they're only at their most powerful at night in the winter, when the moon is high and the air is cold.

Water is a feminine element. These witches are mysterious, intuitive beings who can turn water droplets into ice shards. They are at their strongest at dusk in autumn.

The final feminine element is earth. Users desire stability, practicality, and materialism in the physical world, but with the snap of their fingertips, earth witches can wield bullets made of stone. Their power is most potent during sunrise in the spring.

Four of the five elements have weapons at their disposal to easily disarm prey. Together, at their strongest hour, they would be unstoppable—but this would never happen. It can't be midday in the summer and dusk in autumn at the same time. Mamá says the earth can only handle so much magic at once, which is why witches have natural limits and time boundaries.

As a spirit witch, my powers are mental. I have prophetic dreams and can visit the astral plane. Basically, I can feel when something bad is going to happen, and occasionally, I can see snippets of the future when I sleep. These really aren't the greatest powers to have when I'm facing a vampire in real life.

I keep my mind sharp and focus on the world around

me. Darkhaven is a small village in the middle of nowhere. Surrounded by the sea on one side and forest on the others, it is a safe haven for the witch covens that call this home. Humans don't seem to notice when we make our way into the forest for a ritual or to collect plants and berries for elixirs.

The sun won't rise for hours, so I have plenty of time to loop around town, making sure I hit all the spots vampires are likely to search for food. Evernight Bar and Grill is Darkhaven's local restaurant and pub. It's closing in an hour or so, and drunken humans will be stumbling their way through the dimly lit streets like they're meals-on-wheels. Most of the walking blood bags will be lucky to make it home.

The soft smack of heels alerts me.

I am not alone.

I freeze and wait until my moonlit friend makes another noise but realize the stupidity of my actions. I'm now standing in the middle of the sidewalk, open on all sides, just waiting to be attacked.

I reach for my cross and rub the ever-cool metal against the pad of my thumb. The footsteps draw nearer, and my heartbeat increases to ear-piercing levels.

They're close.

I want to call out, to shout some obscenity in a sad attempt at looking vaguely threatening. I grasp my stake, and just as I'm about to yank it free, I falter.

What if a human is walking nearby? How am I going to explain carrying a stake? A *vampire stake*. Thanks to the humans' love for the supernatural, every idiot out walking after sunset knows exactly what weapon to use to kill a vampire. If I risk exposure, Mamá will have my head. Humans can never know vampires and witches exist.

I loosen my grip and spin on my heels, coming face-to-face with—

"Liv?" I whisper.

My best friend since kindergarten is rushing toward me. She's replaced her usual preppy clothes with an outfit that looks like it came straight from my closet. She's dressed in all black and carries her mother's butcher knife in a white-knuckle grasp with both hands. She holds it out before her like it's an atomic bomb that will be triggered by the slightest movement.

"What are you doing here?" I hiss when she makes it to my side. "And put that thing down. Someone might see you running down the street looking like Jason Voorhees. How would we explain that?"

"Michael Myers," she whispers.

"What?"

"Jason Voorhees uses a machete."

I roll my eyes. "Whatever. The point is, you look like a psycho. And a machete would probably be more useful. What do you expect to do with that thing? It can't penetrate their sternum."

"Well, I was kind of hoping I wouldn't have to actually use it." Her eyes are wide, and there are dark circles below her usually well-rested gaze. Seeing her look so exhausted softens my approach.

"Why are you here?" I ask.

"I knew you'd do something stupid like this."

"Like what? I always take patrol."

"Never alone!" Liv counters.

Finally, she lowers her weapon to her side and spins in a full circle twice until she's sure no one has followed us here.

"Do you realize how ridiculous you look right now?" I

hold back a chuckle, which only angers her. She smacks me hard on the arm, and I overdramatically feign discomfort.

"You've been talking about this *dark presence* for weeks now. I just knew you'd sneak out and try to take things into your own hands. You're too reckless. That's why Tatiana won't take you seriously. She probably knew you'd sneak out."

I wince when she mentions Mamá's name, and I don't miss the way she emphasizes *dark presence*. Like Mamá, Liv doesn't really believe me either.

"If Mamá knew I'd sneak out, how am I here right now?" I counter. "Don't you think she'd throw up some kind of boundary spell or something? You know she'd lock me in my room until I'm forty!"

Liv offers a wicked grin. "She definitely would do that. Remember the time you couldn't even leave your closet until you put away your clothes?"

I snort and steer the conversation back to the point. "You need to go home, Liv."

"You know that's not going to happen."

"You've never trained for this. You could get hurt. Or worse..."

Despite the fact that we're best friends, Liv isn't in my coven. Her mother formed her own coven long ago after too many witches settled in this area. It made more sense to form multiple covens under their own leadership than to form one massive coven under one witch. And unfortunately, Liv's coven doesn't believe in violence. Even though she's a fire witch—arguably one of the strongest elements against vampires—she's never trained to hunt the undead like I have. She could have been a real asset in our war against these creatures.

"I'm a fire witch. I'll be fine. I'm more worried about you."

I arch a brow. "What do you mean?"

"Ava… Ever since you started having those dreams, you've been—"

"Look, I'm fine, okay? And we haven't the time to discuss this now anyway. If you're going to come with, then you need to be quiet, stay alert, and do whatever I say exactly when I say it. Got it?"

She nods slowly. I can't miss her fear.

"I won't tell anyone about this if you want to go home," I add.

Her brow furrows. "Let's go." She pushes past me and trudges down the sidewalk. I'm not sure where she's going— and honestly, I'm sure she doesn't know either—but I follow beside her.

When we reach the cemetery, she shimmies through the iron gates. I sigh and follow after her. It's time for lesson one in vampire hunting.

"Liv?"

"Hmm?"

"Contrary to just about every supernatural movie ever, vampires don't actually hang out in cemeteries."

She spins to face me, eyes in disbelief. "You sure?"

"They eat the *living*. There's nothing for them here but dusty bones."

"I've seen TV shows where vampires actually live in mausoleums."

I snort. "Well, if you've seen it on TV, it *must* be real!"

She rolls her eyes and nudges her shoulder against mine. Together we stand, side by side, facing the seemingly endless rows of perfectly placed headstones. The dead of Darkhaven reside here—including many witches.

"Where would you have started?" she asks as we dig both our hands into our pockets in search of spare change.

I shrug, finding a few silver coins. I grasp them tightly in my palms and pull them free. "Evernight is a good place to start. It'll close soon, and drunks will be stumbling home."

She nods and pulls free her own bundle of coins. "That would make sense. They're easy targets."

"Exactly," I say. "But since we're already here, we might as well do a quick loop."

She meets my gaze and smiles. Together, we toss our coin offerings to the side of the drive and take our first step past the threshold and into the resting place of the dead. It's customary that we offer something when visiting cemeteries—whether it be baked goods, herb bundles, fresh flowers, or even coins.

The night air is chilly, and Liv shivers beside me. I reach for my cross necklace and run my fingertips over the metal. Already, I am stronger. I glance at Liv, and her neck is bare. I consider loaning her my necklace or maybe my baggie of protection herbs. She needs something to boost her courage.

"Do you have a stake?" I ask.

She shakes her head.

"Maybe you should take mine."

"Keep it. I have fire magic."

I exhale slowly. "Here. Take this." I offer her the horehound and mugwort.

She grabs the baggie and crinkles her nose as she takes a big whiff. "Yuck. I hate the smell of mugwort."

"So do vampires," I lie.

She arches a brow. "Really?"

I nod. "It'll help keep you safe." I don't bother telling her the truth—that the protection spell might fail against the

11

undead. I brought it on the off chance it would actually work.

She considers my words before responding. "Then maybe you should keep it."

I grumble under my breath, hoping the entire night won't go like this. "I have a stake and a cross around my neck. You have a fairly useless kitchen utensil and baby magic."

She scoffs. "I do not have baby magic!"

I grin. I coined the term "baby magic" to refer to any witch inexperienced in the craft of war. Sure, she has control over fire, but without the ability to wield it, she's a mere baby.

We're silent the rest of the way as Liv pretends to be annoyed with me. I run my hands over headstones as we walk and scan our surroundings. I try to think of small talk, but it's no use. I'm too on edge—and so is Liv.

The moon is big and bright above us, hanging in the sky like a welcome beacon. Soon, my coven will perform our monthly full moon ritual. This time, Mamá says I'll lead. As successor, I need to learn to harness my power in front of an audience.

"What are you thinking about?" Liv whispers.

But I don't answer her because I'm overwhelmed by dread. Something within me sparks, and the fear and agony that've been nestled in the pit of my gut rise within me until I'm consumed by it.

My pulse races, my palms sweat, and my knees weaken. Thoughts race through my mind as I stare at the cemetery in disbelief.

She was right.

I yank Liv to the ground, and we lunge for a nearby headstone.

My breath comes in shallow bursts, keeping me alive but

unable to satisfy my desire to stay conscious.

Liv jams her elbow into my side to get my attention. Her lips move, but I don't hear her words. The world around me is darkening as it closes in on me.

All at once, my magic sparks to life, warning me of incoming danger.

Vampires.

TWO

My hands shake as I grip the handle of the butcher knife. Liv dropped it in our scuffle to hide, and I grabbed it before the moonlight could glisten from the blade, betraying our presence. The vampires will know we're here when I want them to—and not a moment sooner.

I keep my eyes focused for them, watching for the slightest movement. We are close enough to lose our lives, but I am confident. I have yet to lose a fight.

Liv peeks over the top of the tombstone we're hiding behind before jumping back and falling on her behind. I place a finger firmly to my lips to hush her as she squirms back to her place beside me.

I'm sure I can hear her heartbeat in the air, and if I can hear it, the vampires can as well. I don't have much time before they pick up our scent or hear the soft noises of our inner-workings, like our lungs expanding to breathe or our hearts pumping blood to various parts of our bodies. Every time I encounter a vampire, I become envious of their still-beating heart. They have all the perks and so few weaknesses. It just isn't fair.

I'm twisting the blade in my hand as I consider my next move. Liv eyes me curiously, her gaze wide with wonder and fear. It's kind of beautiful. Did I look that way on my first hunt?

Sometimes, I wish I was never born a witch. It comes with too much burden and expectation and no real freedom. I wish to be human, to go to a real school and spend the afternoons skipping class to get lattes with friends. I want to crush on my teachers and be asked to a dance by a boy I like. I want to sneak out at night to visit that boy, not to hunt monsters.

With each passing second, I become angrier and more envious of the life I'll never have. And I use that. I use those emotions to catapult me from fearing for my life to telepathically shouting at the vampires that they need to fear for theirs.

"What are we going to do?" Liv whispers.

"We're going to kill them all," I say plainly.

In an instant, I pounce to my feet and charge at the vampires. I don't listen for Liv or wonder if she'll follow my lead. I don't care that I'm reckless and that it could cost me my life. All I can think about is the possibility of a world without vampires. There would be magic and love and freedom and nothing else. I want that world. And to get it, I need to kill them all.

The vampires hear my approach and watch as I run toward them with butcher knife in hand. I'm sure I look comical, and I bet they won't take me seriously. That gives me an advantage over them. Already, they're being dealt the losing hand.

"Well, well, what have we here?" one says after I've skidded to a stop. Liv is beside me, her cheeks flushed from running or from the fire building within her.

I hope my pulse doesn't betray my forced confidence. I need them to fear me—or to at least wonder *if* they should fear me. It's not commonplace for a witch to confront a vampire, especially outnumbered. I'm sure they can sense Liv's inadequacy and my concern for her safety.

A vampire steps forward, putting himself between the others and me. Normally, it is more difficult to determine the leader—the one who poses the greatest threat—but he makes it quite simple. He is taller than the others. His tousled brown hair sits messily atop his head, a just-out-of-bed style I am sure he works hard for. He stares as if he can read straight into one's soul. He has stubble on his jaw, as if he hasn't shaved in days. I find myself wondering how long they have been hunting in *my* village.

He raises his arm as the woman behind him steps forward baring bright-white fangs and dirt-caked fingers. It's almost as though he predicted her temper. I meet her gaze and hold it, challenging her.

The wind picks up, blowing her blond pixie locks from her eyes. Like all vampires, her irises are red, cold, void of life. She stares with the intensity of a killer, and I promise myself I'll end her.

She stands beside her leader, a good half-foot shorter than me. Her thin form shows no muscular build. I am sure I can take her easily. She gives me a knowing smile and licks her lips. Her fangs lengthen as her lip curls upward, and I swallow down the nausea that's quickly building within me.

Hoping to take my enemies by surprise, I slash the butcher knife forward, ripping through skin, before quickly pulling it back. Stumbling backward, the vampire looks down at the long slash across his chest and then growls as we lock eyes. His icy crimson irises burn into me.

My hesitation is all he needs, and with a few long strides, he is standing before me. His hand clasps mine and squeezes. I drop the knife as he yanks my arms back and spins me around.

My back to his chest, he pulls me up against him, lifting my body until his mouth reaches my throat. He digs his fingers into my skin. I wince as his short nails draw blood, and I throw my head back. He drops me as my skull smashes into his nose, and I somersault to safety.

My heart thuds against my chest, but I hear it in my head. Solid, steady beats that make focusing on the task at hand nearly impossible. My breath comes in quick bursts, even though I know I'm fine. I've trained daily for this very moment. I *can* do this. I *will* win.

My gaze darts between the vampires and the ground between us. The butcher knife protrudes from the earth, where I dropped it mere moments ago. The blonde offers a wicked grin. She plans to use Liv's weapon against us. It might not be an effective vampire-killing tool, but I certainly don't want them to have it.

I run for the knife, skidding against the ground in an attempt to outmaneuver the incoming vampire. In the time it took me to decide if I should risk my life for what is probably a useless weapon, the female vampire has already made her decision. She dashes from behind her leader, grabs the knife just as I sink to my knees, and brings it down on me.

Time slows as the blade turns on me. The pointed edge is above me now and rushing closer to my chest as I withdraw the only weapon I have—my stake.

Turning it on its side, I hold it out just before the knife makes impact. Her wrist twists, and the blade scrapes against my silver stake. The clink of metal on metal radiates through my arms and down my spine. The vampire pushes her weapon against mine, and I sink down, my bottom firmly planted against my heels. Sweat dribbles down my forehead; I keep my eyes locked on hers. Briefly, I think about the other vampires and Liv. If I die tonight, I'm condemning her too.

I release a loud groan as the vampire takes a step forward and puts her entire upper body strength against our blades. Under her strength, the butcher knife snaps, falling to the ground in pieces. Her reaction time is faster than mine. While I'm still dragging my gaze back to hers, she's already reaching for my neck.

The tips of her dirt-caked fingernails tease the throbbing vein in my neck. She smiles, and I call upon spirit.

My element surges through me, and as it sparks from my fingertips, I say, "*Incendia.*" The word escapes my lips in a whisper, but it's enough to call upon fire magic. The vampire screams, falling backward as she is engulfed in flames.

Spirit witches have a small affinity for each element. It's enough to distract a vampire, but not enough to inflict real harm. I have only seconds to make a choice.

In my fear, I dropped my stake. I dig my nails into the dirt as I grab it now. Quickly, I bring it down, planting it firmly in her chest. Her eyes nearly bulge from their sockets. Each ridge of her rib cage gives way to the magic encased in the stake until the solid silver point penetrates her heart.

Anything pointy could kill a vampire. After all, very few creatures can survive a direct assault to the heart. But a vampire's rib cage is a problem. Their bones are as strong as granite, so it takes a special weapon—like a stake surging with magic and protected by runes—to crush them.

She gasps as her body begins to turn to ash. In these moments, I never know what a vampire feels. Does it hurt to die? Or do they feel relief? Living an immortal life as an undead being isn't for everyone. The price for immortality is watching your loved ones age and die. I'd never want that curse. But I'm not even sure a vampire can *feel* emotions.

In my distraction, her leader flashes before my eyes in a blur, slamming into me. We fall to the ground, but I tighten my grip on my stake. If I am going to die tonight, I am taking him with me. He's the reason they're even here, hunting in this cemetery. I'm sure of it.

I bring my arm back, slamming my elbow into the earth beneath me, and sink my stake into his gut. I wish I could reach his heart from this angle, but I can't. His fangs grow longer as he growls. In a daring move, he releases my arm to grab on to the stake protruding from his body. I wiggle over, bringing my knee up in a sharp jab to his family jewels. While he falters, I escape with my weapon and jump to my feet.

I glance from vampire to vampire. The leader is just beginning to stand, and I need to kill him quickly. He is the strongest and biggest threat. But the third vampire, the one I haven't paid any attention to, has Liv cornered. It takes little effort to make my decision.

Liv's back is to me, giving me a clear shot at the vampire's heart.

I call upon spirit once more and invoke the air element. Suddenly, the winds rush around me, and I focus them as I throw my stake. The element aids my endeavor, strengthening the force behind my weapon. It spins end over end, slicing through the air just before sinking into the vampire's chest. His eyes widen in surprise.

Liv screams as the vampire tumbles over. She reaches for the stake, grunts while pushing it in until the smooth end is parallel with his flesh, and then yanks it free. The vampire turns to dust before he even hits the ground.

The final vampire bares fangs and lunges forward. I jump to the side, and he grazes past me. In a move too fast for my human eyes, he spins around, grabs the loose strands from my bun, and yanks my head backward. I cry out.

Before I can call upon my element, before Liv can protect me with her fire, the vampire sinks his fangs into my neck. He viciously tears through skin, and my screams echo in the night. I blink away the tears that blur my vision as my life-force is drained through a tiny vein in my neck.

Liv is screaming something. Her lips move, but her shouts fall mute upon my ears. All I can hear is the blood rushing to my head, and all I can feel is my stake burning against the palm of my weakening hand. It radiates as if the magic inside knows I'm in trouble, and it's begging to be tapped into.

Caeli.

I mouth the word to call upon the air element and use its strength to jab my elbow backward. The vampire is jolted from me. He stumbles backward, and I tumble to the side, trying to regain my balance. I'm weakened from the blood loss, and I have mere seconds to regain my composure.

By the time I face him, he's already charging me, my blood dripping from his chin and splattering against the ground. Even now, it slides down the curve of my neck. It's a slow, steady stream that will lead me to my death.

He reaches me in the short amount of time it takes me to blink, but I'm already expecting his blood lust to overpower his common sense. I take a strong hold on my stake and angle it so it's perfectly aligned with his heart—he may practically stake himself. I only have one chance to get this right.

Mere steps before he reaches me, he is engulfed in flames. Long, flowing streams of fire cascade all around him. I watch in awe as Liv slowly walks toward us, her arms outstretched, waves of fire shooting from her palms. He is enveloped in her magic, and a vampire is no match against a witch's more powerful weapon.

Liv falls to the ground beside me, the fire from her hands extinguished. She's breathing heavily and looking every bit utterly exhausted. This was likely the first time she's ever called upon fire so ferociously.

I cover my neck wound with my hand. Blood gushes from the wound with each breath I take. The steady beats of my heart are sending me spiraling down to a certain death.

My throat is coarse. It hurts to speak, to move. Somewhere in the fight, ribs were broken, and with each inhalation, the pain stabs at my side.

"Oh my Goddess!" Liv shrieks when she reaches my side. "Your neck, Ava . . . It's really bad!"

"Your . . . fire," I whimper.

Understanding my request, she yanks my hand away from my wound and uses her magic to cauterize the flesh. This is a temporary solution to what will become a permanent problem if I don't get an actual healing elixir into me soon. With each second that passes, the healing potion Mamá prepares becomes more ineffective. Witches aren't miracle workers, and we need time on our side.

"We need to get you to Tatiana," Liv says. Mamá has always been known to the magical community in Darkhaven as an experienced healer. In fact, witches from all over come to buy her elixirs. If anyone can heal me, it's Mamá.

But first, she needs to know I'm not really in my room, that I've disobeyed her, and that I endangered not only my life but also the life of a witch from another coven. I'm so going to be spelled to my room until I'm thirty.

I nod as I try to sit up, and the blood rushes to my head, making me want to keel over and vomit. My stomach aches, the nausea overturning my control.

"I don't feel well," I say.

"Are you kidding? You almost died! Of course you don't feel well," Liv says.

I wobble on my feet as we stand, and she wraps my arm around her neck, balancing my weight against her own.

"If only I were an air witch, we could fly home," Liv jokes.

"If you were an air witch, we'd both be dead."

We take a couple of steps forward, and I nearly fall over as I dry heave. I choke in a breath.

"Something's wrong."

"Let's just get you home," Liv says. "You're going to be okay."

"Liv... This feeling isn't from blood loss," I whisper as I scan our surroundings.

She sucks in a sharp breath. "Please don't say what I think you're going to say."

"There are more..."

Somewhere, probably in this cemetery, probably watching us even now, there are more vampires. Spirit is warning me of the danger that lurks within the shadows, and it knows Liv and I are far too weak to fight.

Slowly, we put distance between us and the fight scene. Each step we haven't encountered yet another vampire means we're safer than we were even seconds earlier. Praying we can make it the couple thousand or so it takes to reach home, I count each step we take.

Unfortunately, I only make it to ten.

THREE

From the shadows, he emerges. Tall, broad-shouldered, with dark skin and cold eyes, he confidently strides toward us. His head is shaved to the scalp, and the moonlight shines brightly off his smooth skin. I find myself wondering how I didn't notice him before. He's so tall and muscular, I'm sure there isn't even a mausoleum he could hide behind.

I swallow the knot that forms in my throat and straighten, taking a step away from Liv. I withdraw my stake and hold it firmly in my hand. My stance is threatening and, hopefully, doesn't show the immense pain I'm in after everything that just happened.

"You're not welcome here," I say.

He smiles. His teeth are shiny and white, with two perfect fangs protruding from his lips. When he finally speaks, his words twist around my neck like a noose.

"Is a cemetery not the resting place for the dead?" he asks. His voice is deep and firm. I'm taken aback by his wit. It's not often a vampire is humorous. I almost feel bad for the fact that I'm replaying his death over and over again in my mind.

"Leave Darkhaven and never return," I order. I grasp my stake tighter and move my arm upward so the weapon is showcased before me. I may be weak, but I'm still standing and armed. I'm still a witch who hunts vampires, and I did just kill his allies while he watched from the shadows.

Does this vampire have a death wish?

Better yet, do I?

He takes another step forward. Several feet still separate us, but with each passing second, the monster continues to corner us. I need to make a decision quickly. Either we fight and risk death, or I convince him to leave, and then once I'm at full strength and Liv is safely at home, I hunt him down.

"Do you often offer free passes to vampires?" he asks.

I don't speak. He and I both know why I'm not attacking. I'm weak from blood loss, and I'm not sure I can withstand the stabbing pain from my broken ribs that shoots through my side when I move too quickly. I may not be at my full strength tonight, but I will be soon.

"Choose your words carefully, vampire."

He smiles. "Is it not your job, little huntress, to force me out of this world—or, at the very least, out of your village?" he asks.

I don't respond because I'm mulling over his words. This is the first time I've ever really spoken to a vampire. Most have no interest in talking things out, and no one has ever called me "little huntress" before.

I find myself considering his age. He could be the same age as Papá if he were alive. I've never seen a vampire as old as my parents.

Liv must take my silence as her cue to assist me, because she steps forward so we're side by side and holds out her hand. A fireball forms in her palm, and it remains there, bouncing up and down, over and over again. She keeps her gaze on the vampire before us, a wicked grin spreading across her usually calm face.

"We may be weakened by your friends, but we have enough to end you," I threaten.

With just the simple flick of her wrist and the flash of a fireball, the vampire begins to recede into the shadows. He doesn't need to tell me this isn't over. I can see it written across his face. He'll return to Darkhaven, and when he does, he'll come for me. With the help of Liv, I killed his friends and forced his retreat with his tail between his legs. His pride will get the best of him sooner or later. By then, I'll be healed and ready for a fight.

"I'll see you again, little huntress," he whispers before disappearing.

I exhale slowly and collapse onto Liv. I glance over at her, our gazes meeting, and for a brief moment in time, we just smile at each other.

We did it.

We made it.

We survived, and the world is short three more vampires.

It's not lost on us that killing one vampire creates a ripple effect. We saved lives tonight.

This is the first time Liv went on a hunt, and by the excitement in her eyes, I'm not sure it'll be the last.

She holds me up, pulling me tight, and we trudge through the village toward my home, where Mamá is waiting for us. Over and over, I replay my apology to her. She will be furious, and I will be grounded—probably spelled to my room with no chance of escape.

Even though I know exactly what Mamá will say, I'm unsure of how Liv's parents will react. Her coven is notorious for peaceful philosophies. I'm sure sneaking out of the house to hunt vampires with a friend is absolutely unacceptable. I pray they won't be too hard on her. After all, she was just trying to save my life.

❖

Liv kicks the door shut behind us, and it slams a little too loudly. We both freeze, waiting for what we're sure is inevitable. After a few seconds pass, our shoulders settle, and I saunter over to my bed. But the moment I fall onto it and finally take a breath, my bedroom door opens and Mamá appears.

I actually believed we had gotten away with it. I mean, sure, my neck looks like a dog tore through a bag of treats, but I could hide it with clothes and makeup—but in time, in the form of a scar, it would become a daily reminder of the vampire who got away.

Correction: the vampire I let escape . . .

"Explain this right now, *mija*," Mamá says. I can tell by her directness that lying will only land me in purgatory for an eternity, so I come clean and hope she goes easy on us.

"*Yo tenia que hacerlo*, Mamá!" She must understand that I had no choice. I *had* to do this! She might not take my gut instincts seriously yet, but I do. Something is coming, and it is my duty to protect Darkhaven.

"It's my fault, Mrs. López!" Liv says, cutting in.

I appreciate her attempt to take sole responsibility for my actions tonight, but even Mamá will find a way to turn this back onto me. She'll definitely see through Liv's lie. I mean, she *always* sees through mine. I'm not quite sure why I ever believed I could get away with sneaking out. I guess it just didn't matter enough. The only thing I cared about was finding a way to make this . . . feeling stop.

"It is your responsibility, *mija*, to protect this village—not to endanger it. You risked your friend's life tonight. That is *imperdonable*."

"But it was my idea!" Liv shouts.

"*Silencio!*" Mamá shouts.

Liv bows her head and falls back onto my bed. We sit side by side, both afraid to look Mamá in her eyes.

"Do your parents know where you are, *niña*?"

Liv shakes her head.

"Do you want to die tonight?" Mamá says, and I'm not sure if she's asking if that was our original plan or if she's letting us know she's happy to commit the deed.

Liv's parents are quiet, calm, happy people made of sunshine, flowers, and good intentions. I get my recklessness and fiery temper from Mamá. I shoot Liv a look that tells her to be quiet and let me handle this. She is inexperienced when it comes to a ruthless parent.

"*Lo siento*, Mamá." I apologize because there's nothing left to say. She won't accept that the reason I disobeyed her and went hunting is because she refuses to believe my gut. I *know* something bad is going to happen, and she's forcing me to simply sit down and shut up and wait for it to happen. I just can't do that. Mamá did not raise a daughter who can stand down. She raised a fighter, a survivor, a *defender* of those who cannot protect themselves. That pretty much describes almost all the population of Darkhaven. Those who aren't blissfully unaware humans are witches in a coven that resents violence. Darkhaven is the perfect place for vampires to feast on; it should have a twenty-four-hour patrol team.

"*Hablaremos de esto más tarde*," Mamá says, and I sink

a little farther into my bed. The last thing I want to do is talk about this later.

I nod, gaze still on the floor.

"*Estás herido?* Are you hurt?" Mamá repeats herself in English so Liv understands her question. She used to hate doing this, but she cannot stop herself from speaking Spanish, her first language. Now, most of our conversations are like this—some English, some Spanish. I'm not sure she even notices it anymore. She probably thinks she's always speaking just one or the other.

"I'm tired," Liv says.

"You used too much *la magia*," Mamá explains. "You're a couple of seventeen-year-old girls. *Eres un novato.*" I'm glad Liv doesn't speak Spanish, because being called a novice is the last thing she needs right now, especially considering the only reason we're alive is because she stepped up and scared away the final vampire.

My mind flashes back to the moment I let him go. I'm ashamed to have done that. For all I know, he's out killing little kids right now while I'm safely inside my home. Well, *safely* could be argued. I'm not sure Liv and I are safe around Mamá tonight.

"*Fui mordido*," I whisper. Admitting I was bitten is harder than I thought it'd be. I'd rather take a dagger to the gut than admit to Mamá that she was right, that I shouldn't have patrolled alone, that I shouldn't have brought a novice to hunt vampires. I made so many mistakes tonight, I'm not quite sure how I survived the ordeal.

Mamá covers her shock with her hand and rushes to me. "Did you drink?"

I shake my head so hard it makes me dizzy. I cringe at

the relief that washes over Mamá's face. If I did drink the vampire's blood, I would begin my transition, and then what? What would she do? What does her relief mean? Would she kill me, her only child, just because I've become what she hates? I wouldn't want to become a bloodsucking monster, but I certainly don't want to die tonight either.

"*Déjame ver*," she says.

I tilt my head to the side to expose my neck. I'm not sure what it looks like, and Mamá's face doesn't exactly give away how serious my injury truly is. As she assesses the damage, I wonder how many times she's been on the other side of one of these wounds. I haven't heard many stories of witches being bitten by vampires, so I'm not sure what the protocol is. If I were to have ingested the vampire's blood, would she wait until after my transition to kill me? Or would she kill me before I change in a halfhearted attempt to save my soul?

She inspects my wound with her hands. Her fingers are warm and welcoming, unlike her steely glare and harsh words. After a few seconds, she steps back and nods at me. She can create a potion to heal my wound quickly. I may not even scar this time.

I glance down at my hands. They're covered with tiny battle wounds. I remember how I got each one, and I can *feel* them too. I think it's a weird survivor's curse. When I close my eyes, I know where they all are. I can even sense the shape of them, like the long, thick one on my left calf; it has a small part that sticks out from the center. I got that one when I tried to scale a fence and only succeeded in catching my leg at the pointed tip. I feel like I have at least a hundred war wounds all over my body, but I'm sure that's not the real number.

"Very smart to use your fire magic," Mamá says to Liv.

"Thank you," she responds.

"How many vampires have you slain before?" Mamá asks, and my stomach sinks. The silence seems to stretch on for hours as she waits for Liv to respond. I don't need to be a mind reader to know what's happening here. Liv is scared to be honest, but she doesn't want to lie either. Mamá is patient, like a shark that swims 'round and 'round a fallen diving tank, just waiting for the right moment to strike. Liv will be the first to break, so she may as well get it over with. I give her a look that tells her to be honest.

"This was my first time," Liv says, shame evident in her downward lashes.

Mamá exhales sharply, and fear strikes through me like a bullet through flesh. It stings, and the pain permeates far and wide. I'm not sure I'll ever recover from her anger. Like my many scars, her disappointment from this night will be something I'll remember forever.

"*Cómo pudiste ser tan estúpida?*" She doesn't wait for me to respond before returning her attention to Liv. "Have you been bitten, child?"

Liv shakes her head.

"Good. Come now."

We stand in unison and follow closely behind Mamá until we reach our altar room. The room is large and encompasses much of the second floor of our home. Large bay windows help to flood the room in moonlight, but during the day, the sun bathes the many rows of plants with much-needed sunlight. There's even a large walk-in closet full of plants that can't handle all the light.

Every herb imaginable is found in this place. I remember the first time I came in here and wasn't treated like a child.

Every time prior to that moment, Mamá would swat me from the room. She told me the altar room was no place for a child. Eventually, I was old enough to study herb magic, and Mamá explained all the magical properties of each plant she nurtures. Even now, as she walks to her altar and begins placing various herbs in a mortar, I know she's reaching for herbs like rosemary, thyme, amaranth, Angelica leaves, barley grass, bay leaves, lemon balm, and others.

She crushes the mixture while I bring a vial of a light amber-colored liquid to Liv. I hold it out to her, and she takes it from me, eyeing it curiously.

"Peppermint tea. We brew it regularly," I say.

She nods like she knows what it is, but she doesn't. Her mother doesn't train her to wield her magic the way Mamá teaches me. I've been training to avenge Papá since he was killed by a vampire. Liv got lucky tonight, but I'm not sure she'll be that lucky next time. In a village crawling with supernaturals, Liv really should learn how to be a witch.

"It's a powerful base for a healing elixir," I confirm. I don't have to face Mamá to know she's smiling while eavesdropping. She's been training me to harness my spirit magic for a long time. Our powers are not physical, like a fire witch's. We're natural healers and psychics with minimal control over the elements.

"Are you going to drink it?" Liv asks.

I nod. "You should too."

"But I wasn't bitten. I'm fine."

"You don't know that for sure. I don't remember taking a hit to the side, but I'm certain I've broken a rib. In the heat of the battle, adrenaline overpowers your feelings. It's better to drink the potion and not need it than to skip it and have regrets."

Liv shrugs. "I guess."

"We'll add Mamá's herb mixture to it, let it rest for a minute while we infuse it with spirit magic, and then we can drink it. We should feel much better in just a few hours."

I take the vial from Liv's hand and walk over to Mamá. She sets down her pestle while I unscrew the top from the vial. She places her hand over my own, and together, we hold the tiny glass jar above the mortar. Closing our eyes, we chant, fueling the elixir with spirit magic to aid its ability to heal wounds quickly. When done, we open our eyes to see the amber-colored liquid glowing ever so slightly. We don't have much time now. In one small splash, the peppermint tea mixes with the crushed herbs. Mamá swirls it together before emptying it into two small chalices. I take one and hand the other to Liv.

"Shall we?" I say, offering mine to clink.

Before Liv can place glass to glass, Mamá says, "*Este no es el momento, mija.*" Always the buzzkill.

I pull back, a bit ashamed I was trying to make light of the situation, and swallow down the elixir. Liv follows suit, scrunching her nose as soon as the liquid hits her tongue. Even though the base is peppermint tea, by the time Mamá mixes in the crushed herbs, the taste changes. The flavor is definitely not something one enjoys or would drink regularly.

Already, the solution is working its way through my body. The magic seeps into my core and fans out, threading with each fiber of me. It works its way to my side, where the ache of broken ribs dulls. I reach for my neck, and the burned flesh feels smoother under my fingertips.

"You must sleep now," Mamá says as I yawn.

"What about Liv?" I ask. My eyelids are heavy. Mamá must have added another herb to help us sleep.

"Come, *niñas*," she says, guiding us to my room.

The moment my head hits the pillow, I'm overwhelmed by the magic that's eagerly working its way through me. It reaches even the darkest parts of me, where lingering thoughts of doubt and dreams of future dread reside.

FOUR

The sunlight is warm against my skin. I'm sitting in a field of wildflowers, and I'm young—somewhere between four and five years old. I don't know the day or even the year, but I do know that I'm safe.

The only reason I know it's not real is because Papá is here. He's alive, happy.

It always begins this way.

He smiles at me. His jaw is strong, sharp. A dusting of hair covers his chin—some of it black, some gray. His eyes are soft with lines edging each as he smiles down at me.

"*Te amo, mija.*" His voice is deep but gentle as he tells me he loves me.

In this moment, I believe we'll be safe forever. I don't know about the demons of the world or understand the growing sensation within me that's screaming at me to leave this place. I now know spirit was warning me about the vampires, about Papá's demise, but I was too young to understand it then. I was too young to help him.

I open my tired eyes, and I'm back in my room. I often dream of the night Papá died. It's part of the spirit witch curse. My affinity isn't for control over the elements—it's for the mind, the soul, and the memories and instincts that make living the definition of hell.

There's a soft bustling noise coming from downstairs. I'm sure my house is swarming with people as my coven prepares for tonight's full moon ritual. Soon, Mamá will come looking for me, and if I'm not ready when our high priestess arrives, there will be hell to pay.

I groan and sit on the edge of my bed. I sink my face into the palms of my hands, rest my elbows on my thighs, and run my fingers through my matted hair.

"I can do this," I say aloud.

My voice is soft, unsure. I have been mentally preparing myself for this moment ever since I decided to sneak out. Of course, I was hoping I *wouldn't* get caught...

With one last, quick exhalation, I rise and walk into my bathroom. My muscles are stiff from last night's fight, but breathing no longer causes extreme agony. Mamá's elixir certainly worked its magic on me while I slept.

I stand in front of the mirror and stare at my reflection. I'm exhausted, but I don't look it. That's the beauty of ingesting a healing potion. My skin isn't dull, my eyes aren't sunken, and those tiny bags that have plagued my existence ever since I sensed the incoming darkness are finally gone.

I pull back my hair, brushing it to one side with my fingers, and wince when they catch in a tangle. I gnaw on my lower lip as I assess the damaged goods. The potion did a fairly good job healing my wound, but a scar remains. I was silly to think Mamá's magic could completely erase the two puncture marks and the crescent-shaped spattering of tiny teeth indents.

I stand straight and allow my hair to fall back into place. When it hangs over my shoulders, you can't see the scar. But I can feel it. And it feels like failure. I wasn't defeated last night, but it sure feels like I was. I should be happy that Liv and I survived and took out three vampires, but I can't focus on that. I can only focus on my mistake.

My heart sinks every time I think about the vampire I let escape. His crimson eyes haunt me even now. When I close my eyes, I see his.

I shake away the vision of him staring back at me and try to refocus on my own reflection in the mirror, but all I see is myself with crimson irises, pale skin, and a bloodstained chin. I'm smiling, and my teeth are tinted pink with the blood of a fresh kill. Fangs hang prominently, and I run my tongue over them, enjoying the way they feel when they scrape against flesh.

I curse and smash a balled fist against my glass mirror. It breaks under my fury. Small chunks fall from the wall and land on the countertop. Cracks spread outward from the point of impact, fanning into a spider web that distorts my reflection.

Good. I don't want to look at myself anymore. Even so, I find myself focusing harder, trying to make the pieces of me fit again.

Shaking my head, I finally tear my gaze away from the mirror. I can't keep staring at this reflection. It's not me. The girl who looks back with a hint of deviousness in her eyes is *not me.*

My hand aches, so I check the damage, choosing to focus on the physical rather than my mental distress. Small slashes are scattered across my skin, but the wounds aren't deep. They're more of an annoyance than a real concern. They'll scar and become further evidence of that horrible day.

I swipe the shards of glass into the waste bin and rinse off my hand before stripping and stepping into the shower. As the water swirls down the drain, I stare at it as if I could be hypnotized into a better place. Perhaps a beach? I close my eyes and imagine the grains of sand beneath my feet. The air is heavy with mist and a hint of salt. Seagulls flock in the distance. My toes burrow as I walk closer to the water, and I keep walking until waves splash at my heels.

Eyes open, I'm back in my bathroom. I rest my palms against the wall to support my weight and watch the water pool at my feet. I wonder how long I can stand here like this before someone comes looking for me.

✦

After I've finished getting ready, I set out to find Liv. She and I need to talk about the events of last night before we inform her parents that I'm a horrible influence on their perfect daughter. I cross my fingers with hope that Mamá hasn't already called them.

I tiptoe to our guest bedroom and peek inside—only to find it empty.

"Liv?" I whisper as I enter the room and close the door behind me.

The bed is made, so I can't tell if someone has recently slept in it. Liv is a guest in our house; she would have made the bed after she woke.

In search of more clues, I tiptoe over to the bathroom and knock on the door. No one responds. I whisper her name, but again, no one responds. Feeling confident I'm alone in the room, I twist the knob and peer inside. The room is empty— so is the trash can. I saunter back into the hallway, closing the door to our guest suite behind me.

Has Liv been sent home already? We haven't even been

able to talk about what happened last night or how she should break it to her parents that she killed a vampire while on an ill-advised patrol. I don't have to be a spirit witch to foresee their disappointment in both her choices and our friendship. They will not be pleased with her decision to hunt last night because they're all about coexisting.

Peaceful relationships might work in the movies, but not in Darkhaven. That realization hits home every time. I wish Darkhaven were the place we could all get along. If it were, Mamá and I wouldn't be alone in this house.

Exhaling slowly and a bit overdramatically, I prepare to face the inevitable. I take the stairs two at a time and stop at the landing. Spinning on my toes, I follow the smell of breakfast, noting how empty each room is as I make my way deeper into the house. I'm surprised it's not busier. I could have sworn I heard a commotion downstairs while I was getting ready. Our coven mates should be here. After the events of last night, I slept in, and now we're mere hours from the ritual.

"*Buenos dias*, Mamá," I say when I enter the kitchen. It's not exactly morning anymore, but I did just wake. The greeting seems fitting.

She doesn't respond, and my mood instantly spoils. I wasn't in the best mood to begin with, so I really don't want to deal with a lecture. I need high spirits for tonight's full moon ritual.

I glance at the clock. I have just enough time to eat and meditate before the ritual. There really isn't enough time for a lecture, and I hope Mamá knows that.

"*Yo preparé el desayuno*," Mamá says, and I inhale deeply, trying to see if my sense of smell can detect what she cooked before she tells me. My stomach grumbles. She made my favorite. Maybe she's not mad after all.

"*Gracias*, Mamá," I say, thanking her.

I open the cabinet to find a plate and peer around the room as I close the door. We're alone. For now. I pile a healthy serving of chorizo and eggs and fruit onto my plate.

"*Quieres tortillas?*" she asks. Mamá prefers to eat her eggs with tortillas, but I don't. She asks me if I want some every morning, without fail, even though I always say no. The thought makes me smile.

"No. *Gracias.*"

We eat in silence, and with each passing second, the questions begin to pile up. Where is Liv? Did she go home last night, or did her parents pick her up this morning? Did Mamá tell them what happened? Are they angry with her—or with me? Do they blame Mamá for my escape? And where is everyone else? Our coven should be preparing for the ritual. *Abuela*, my grandma and the high priestess of our coven, should be here.

But I'm too scared to ask these questions. I'm almost too scared to speak at all, for Mamá is not known for her silence.

"I'm sorry I disappointed you, Mamá," I say finally, after an unbearable amount of time has passed and we can't possibly sit in silence any longer without me losing my mind.

"*Lo sé*," she says.

That's it? That's all she's going to say? That she knows? My frustration is boiling within me, and it's only a matter of time before it bubbles over.

"*Donde esta* Liv?" I ask. If she's not here, where is she? Mamá must know.

She doesn't answer. I suppose she doesn't need to. Liv's gone home. Where else would she be? But I want to talk about it, and I want to talk about what happened last night. I'm sure Mamá knows that, which is why she's ignoring me now. She doesn't like talking about the dark feeling I have, because she doesn't sense it. She thinks I'm young, a novice. If she hasn't foreseen it, then I couldn't have either. She thinks I'm misinterpreting the dreams and my feelings, and that makes me so angry. She gives me no credit for all I do for Darkhaven. I've killed dozens of vampires on my patrols. I might have saved hundreds of lives!

"*No puedes estar enojado conmigo para siempre!*" I shout.

Mamá drops her fork. The metal clanks against her plate, and the noise radiates through our silent home. I sink a little farther into my chair.

"*Perdóneme?*" she asks. "What did you just say to me?"

"You can't stay mad at me forever, Mamá," I say, repeating myself.

She reaches across the table, her hand striking out far too quickly for my tired eyes. The moment her palm makes impact against my cheek, tears begin to burn, but I refuse to cry. Instead, I feign shock, disbelief that she would slap me— even if I did deserve it.

"Don't you ever again speak to me that way. You are a child. You do not tell me what I can and cannot do," she hisses.

"*Lo siento,*" I whisper, apologizing.

"After our ritual, you will answer for your disobedience, *mija*. I told you not to go hunting. You did not listen!"

"Neither did you," I say softly.

"What did you say?"

I can practically feel the anger in her words. I'm pushing boundaries I should never even touch, but I can't help it. I'm hurt and angry that she doesn't trust my power enough to believe me. That stings more than my reddened cheek.

"I told you about the darkness, Mamá. You didn't listen to me!"

"*Eres un niña! Que puedes saber?*" she shouts.

Finally, she's honest with me. It has nothing to do with believing me and everything to do with the fact that *she* didn't foresee darkness so there must not be anything to worry about. I can't possibly be stronger than her. Well, I may be a child, but I'm a strong witch, and I know when spirit is speaking to me.

"You will not blame this on me, *niña*," she seethes.

"I'm not blaming you, but you have to understand why I didn't listen to you. Something is coming, Mamá, and it is my duty to protect this village and our coven." I use her words from last night against her. It's a petty move, but my pride is wounded.

"I don't want to talk about this, *mija*," Mamá says sternly.

"But Mamá—"

"*Cállate!* Go prepare for the ritual," she orders, and there is no point in arguing.

Without a word, I nod and walk down a long hallway and step into a small room, closing the door behind me. I inhale deeply as I walk through a cloud of sage smoke. During each esbat, Mamá cleanses our home and ritual room, leaving fresh sage burning all night. The smell is overwhelming to some, but I love it. It feels like magic, and magic is empowering.

Mamá already dressed the room just as she does for every esbat, a celebratory time for witches. The air is filled with sage, and rose petals and mint leaves trail the floor against the walls. Crystals and herb bundles clutter the altar. The room's magic feels like it's seeping into my skin.

I walk straight for the corner meditation area. Runes for

magical guidance, psychic awareness, and spiritual protection are painted on the walls that frame a plush cushion.

Sitting cross-legged, I glance around the room. Before I begin my meditation, I try to clear my mind of lingering thoughts and negativity. Meditating immediately after an argument isn't always easy, but I don't have time to simply walk off the fight and come back later. Our ritual will begin soon, and I need to be ready.

I close my eyes, clear my thoughts, and stow away the doubts to be confronted another day. One by one, in ascending order, my chakras begin to open.

My root chakra glows bright red and is found at the base of my spine. It governs my connection to the world and my fundamental needs, like food and shelter.

I rub the tips of my index fingers with my thumbs, concentrating on the soft sensation that radiates from that spot every time I circle my fingertips round and round. I imagine myself being connected to Mother Earth, her power flowing through me, giving me strength to survive the coming hours.

My sacral chakra glows bright orange and rests just below my naval. It is intimately involved with my creative process and imagination. Mamá believes my sacral chakra is unbalanced and that's why I'm foreseeing darkness.

I gently caress my hands together, holding them out directly in front of my sacral chakra. Even though I find no imbalance, I spend extra time here just to appease Mamá later.

My solar plexus chakra glows bright yellow and sits just above my naval. This chakra has an important role in mental and spiritual awareness. Without balance, embracing and understanding experiences would be difficult.

Raising my arms, I place my hands parallel to my solar

plexus, letting my fingers intertwine. I focus on my naval opening, allowing the incense in the room to heal my inner turmoil over last night's disappointment.

Keeping my eyes closed, I stop for a moment and inhale deeply. The sage's smoke flows through me.

My heart chakra is by far the hardest to open. It glows bright green and is located at the center of my cardiovascular system. The heart is intimately connected to the organs around it and is crucial to my survival. But on a spiritual level, an unbalanced heart chakra makes it difficult to form emotional connections. Ever since I lost Papá, I have had to regularly realign my heart chakra. His death left me closed off to others—something I struggle with daily.

To realign my heart chakra, I lower my left hand to my knee and my right to just below my breastbone. Inhaling deeply and slowly, I envision the tangled mess and smooth out the nicks. I smile from the familiar inner tingling of a realigned chakra.

My throat chakra glows bright blue and, naturally, is located in my throat. This chakra governs self-expression and communication; a blockage can cause emotional isolation and the inability to effectively express feelings. Usually I have no issues conveying my thoughts, but after last night's blunder and this morning's argument, I can feel it growing increasingly more unbalanced.

After imagining the constricted muscles moving freely, I am able to easily move on to my favorite chakra.

The third eye chakra glows bright indigo and lies between my eyebrows. This chakra is in charge of insight and intuition on both spiritual and mundane levels.

As a spirit user, I've always been able to connect easily

with my third eye, the source of a psychic's power. This chakra aids me in my prophetic dreams, even if Mamá doesn't think I'm strong enough to experience a real vision.

No alignment is needed. My third eye opens and closes easily and on command. I am connected to it in ways I can't quite articulate to Mama or anyone else. So I move on to my final chakra.

My crown chakra glows bright purple and sits atop my head. This chakra is arguably the most important one, because without every other chakra balanced, the crown chakra cannot serve as my connection to the world—both physical and spiritual. A healthy crown chakra creates a sense of well-being, peace, and confidence.

With my chakras open, cleansed, and realigned, I compel them to close, one by one.

By the time I've finished, Mamá comes for me as if she could sense my meditation completion.

"It is time," she says.

FIVE

Mamá enters the room dressed in a burgundy cloak—traditional witch attire for rituals—and closes the door. In her hands she holds another cloak. This one is meant for me.

"Bring me the sage," she says as I stand.

I carry the burning bundle of white sage from the altar and bring it to Mamá. I wave it back and forth, up and down the length of her body, cleansing her aura as preparation for the ritual. When I'm finished, I hand her the sage, and she uses it to cleanse my aura just as I used it on her. Cleansing with sage is essential to our rituals. We cannot enter circle with negative energy.

"*Quítate la ropa*," Mamá says, and I nod as I begin removing my clothes.

Tonight, she is not my mother. She is the daughter-in-law to our high priestess—Abuela, my grandma. Mamá is the successor to leadership of our coven, and it is her duty to ensure I become high priestess one day too.

My throat is in knots, even though I finished my chakra cleansing mere minutes ago. I swallow down my nerves and ignore the goose bumps that form. I brush off the physical side effects of anxiety and continue prepping for our ritual.

Mamá covers my naked body with the cloak and buttons it closed from breastbone to midthigh. When finished, she spins me around and places a bowl of dried rose petals in my hand. She twists my hair into a long braid, and I hand her petal after petal as she threads the pieces of flower with my hair.

"*Hemos terminado*," Mamá says, and I nod my understanding. We're finished prepping for the ritual, which means it's time to begin.

Turning on her heel, she leads us out of the room. I glance out the window as we pass. Those not privy to our witchy ways are continuing on with their lives. The distant amber lights of humans in households light up the night. I envy them. Humans never fear for their lives the way witches do. Ignorance truly is bliss.

We step onto the back porch. Our property borders a ten-acre nature preserve, and that small forest outlines our backyard clearing. It hides our rituals from neighbors and offers the idea that we're truly in the middle of nowhere. If we could whisk away to complete our rituals, we would, but a gathering of people looks less suspicious in someone's backyard than in the middle of the woods.

In the middle of the small clearing, our coven mates stand in a circle. Thirteen witches in total stand arm's length from each other. I shiver at the sight of them. They're perfectly illuminated by moonlight, and they stand within a circular barrier made of moonstones. The opalescent color of the crystals reflects the moonlight perfectly. They shimmer, and even glow, in the night. We use these crystals for every moon ritual as our way of honoring the moon's strength and power.

At the very center of the circle, there is an altar carved from a one-hundred-year-old oak tree that had to be cut down one year. We were devastated to lose such a precious gift from Mother Earth, but we didn't let her sacrifice go in vain. We kept the stump and use it in every ritual.

Even now, it is adorned with various ritual tools—something to represent each element: crystals for earth, candles for fire, incense for air, a chalice for water, and a small cauldron for spirit. Two other items decorate the top of our ritual altar: a bundle of sage, which remains lit and smoking throughout the duration of our ritual to continuously cleanse our space, and a large moonstone sphere to represent the moon.

I'm so distracted by the sight, I don't realize Mamá has already entered the circle or that everyone is patiently waiting for me. I hasten my pace and reach the high priestess of our coven.

"*Hola,* Abuela," I say as I face my paternal grandma.

"*Niña,*" she says in an informal greeting.

There is an athame in her hand—the one we use for every ritual. The handle is sleek and black, and the blade is long, double-edged, and shiny silver in color. We've had this ritual tool in our family for generations. Abuela passed it down to Papá, who left it to Mamá and me when he died. Abuela wields it now, but one day, it will be my responsibility to wield it properly.

"How do you enter?" she asks, holding the tip of the blade to my throat.

"With perfect love and perfect trust," I reply. This is how we enter every circle ritual.

She lowers the blade, kisses my cheek, and steps aside. I enter the circle and stand beside Mamá. Abuela returns to her place beside us. Three generations of López witches stand side by side, ready to worship the moon's power.

"Full moons have forever been a mystical time of

connecting with our spiritual, sacred selves," Abuela says. "As born witches, it is our duty to honor all phases of the moon. The full moon tonight represents the culmination of energy. It is during this time we celebrate the moon's completion. The full moon grants us the opportunity to pave the way for change, to begin again."

I stand strong beside Abuela and Mamá, even though I can't help but miss Papá. Every month, when we pay tribute to the moon's strength, I think of him. He should be here, beside us now, not waiting for us in the afterlife.

"Because the full moon increases psychic and emotional sensitivity, we have been preparing for this ritual since the early morning hours," Abuela says. "You should have completed your meditation to realign your chakras and the sage smudging ritual to cleanse your aura. Do not allow the powerful energy to overwhelm you tonight. Instead, harness it as a gift provided by the moon to improve your lives, to start anew, and to strengthen your connection with spirit."

Abuela glances at me, and my cheeks warm. The only witches who can connect with the spirit element are spirit witches, so I know she added that last bit just for me. Like Mamá, she doesn't quite trust my judgment or instincts. It seems every witch in the village thinks I'm a novice spirit witch.

"Beneath our cloaks, we are sky-clad, for this is the way our ancestors worshiped the moon, the earth, the goddesses, and the gods," Abuela continues. "Tonight, we will bathe in the moonlight and allow the power of the moon to infuse with our mortal beings. She shall replenish us, and we shall release all negativity, for there is nothing better than replacing the darkness within us with magical moonlight."

Holding my hands out to my sides, I close my eyes as I

tilt my head back to face the sky. The moonlight shines over me, and I imagine my mind, body, heart, and soul soaking the luminescent silvery rays.

Sunlight energizes and uplifts me, but moonlight excites something else, something sunlight could never touch. Moonlight awakens my intuitive, spiritual side. This side of me is softer, more receptive to empathy and kindness. After every moon ritual, I'm ready to change the world. Absorbing full moonlight is therapeutic and healing, and it especially nourishes my sacral chakra.

"Chant your intentions aloud. Tell the moon what you wish from her," Abuela says, and the many different voices of our coven mates clutter my mind. I focus on my own intentions, blocking out the wishes of others.

"Allow the moon to shower you with love and strength," she continues. "Focus on your innate psychic abilities and connect with her."

The sudden rush of the elements washes over me. The wind increases, tickling my nose and blowing loose tresses into my eyes. But I don't dare open them, even though I so desperately want to see if the others are connecting to the elements as strongly as I am. The temperature rises, and mist forms. The earth vibrates through my feet, sending shock waves through every fiber of my being. I'm giddy with pleasure, power, and rejuvenated strength.

And then everything stops.

The world is spinning, witches are screaming, and I'm falling to my knees as I break connection with spirit.

Mamá stands before me, but she looks into the distance, jaw open, eyes wide with fear.

Still on all fours, I glance in the same direction. My eyes

adjust to the darkness of the woods—and the several sets of glowing crimson irises that stare back at me.

Vampires.

My coven begins to slowly back away, but Mamá steps forward. The witches form a line of defense behind us as they hold hands, interlocking fingers.

"You're not welcome here," Mamá says.

In all my years, Mamá has never frightened me. She's small, short, and while she does have a fiery temper, her bark is much worse than her bite. The anger she showed me today, when she slapped me into obedience, is the most violence I've ever seen from her. In fact, *she* is the one witch hesitant to send witches from our coven out on regular patrols of Darkhaven to hunt vampires. She might not be as soft as Liv's mother, but rarely does Mamá ever strike fear in my heart.

But she does now, confronting the vampires. Her words are laced in hatred rooted so deeply, I'm sure even she doesn't know when or where or how she ever started hating vampires.

"Leave this place. *Now*," she orders.

I stand, feeling a little woozy from my abrupt disconnect with the elements, but I regain my composure quickly. My hands hang as balled fists at my sides as I scan our surroundings. There's at least a half-dozen vampires approaching us, each with eager smiles. They're waiting for the command—the one that tells them they can charge.

It takes only seconds for me to find their leader. He smiles back at me, his eyes offering me a knowing stare. The vampire I allowed to escape last night fulfilled his promise. He returned, with friends, and is coming for my soul.

My coven mates, dressed nude beneath traditional ritual cloaks, are inexperienced in the craft of war. So many choose not to fight and send me out instead.

My heart sinks a little the moment I realize I'm unarmed. My stake is inside, tucked safely in its box in my bedroom. The witches have joined hands, lending their strength and power to those who can harness it, like the fire witches of our coven.

"Tatiana, Ava, join us," Abuela says from behind.

"*Sigueme, niña*," Mamá says.

She's several steps behind me and reaches the threshold of witches by the time I've reached the altar. I glance over and notice the athame. I have only moments to consider my options. At any moment, the vampires can outmaneuver us by speed alone. The last thing I want my coven to do is break the link to allow me passage. That would weaken them. I could never forgive myself if their demise is due to my actions.

My gaze darts between the athame and the vampires, and I know what I must do.

"*Te quiero*, Mamá," I whisper.

I dash to the altar. Just as I wrap the blessed blade in the palm of my hand, a vampire is by my side. He reaches for the athame, but I was expecting this. Spirit witches have very little control over the elements, but it's a lot easier to call upon fire when there's something nearby to tap into.

I harness energy from the flaming candles atop our altar and use it to command fire. The vampire before me is lit aflame, distracting him long enough for me to sink my athame into his chest, penetrating his heart. His eyes bulge from their sockets as his body turns to dust. I sure do appreciate that vampires clean up after themselves. The last thing witches need is to find ways to dispose of bodies.

I twirl the weapon in my hand, readying myself for another attack. I don't have to turn around to know the witches behind me are readying themselves too. They've interlocked their hands, which will send power surges to those who can wield fire. These vampires attacked us, probably expecting an easy battle, but they have no idea who they're messing with.

I give the vampire leader my full attention. I have no concern for the other vampires. If I'm to die today, I'm making sure I'm bringing my one mistake with me.

I can see the anger in his eyes as the witches begin their attack. One by one, the vampires combust. It brings a smile to my face to see him so very disappointed in his fangy friends. Yet again, he misjudged us.

We make the decision to attack in unison. We charge together, and just as he's about to land his first hit, I drop to my knees, skidding past him. I manage to sink my athame into his ankle. His shock is music to my ears. I spin on my heels to face him again.

We're at eye level now, my assault against his legs bringing him down to his knees. He snarls like an animal and claws at the ground as he runs toward me while on all fours. He slams into me, and I tighten my grip on the athame.

But it's no use.

He clutches my hand within his own viselike grip and slams it repeatedly onto the ground until even my will isn't strong enough to maintain my hold on the weapon. I drop the athame, crying out as the tiny bones in my hand snap.

I stare into his crimson irises, and I see it. He hates me just as much as I hate him. I'm not sure if it's because we're destined enemies or if it's because I wounded his pride last night.

He sinks his fangs into my neck, and I shriek from shock, fear, and pain. My gaze darts at our surroundings as he drains my life-force. The witches have disbanded—some running in a hopeless attempt to save themselves, others fighting and succumbing to the strength of these monsters.

Almost as soon as it began, it's over. The vampire sits up, resting his weight against my torso, and smiles down at me with a bloodstained chin. It's *my blood* that coats his skin and stains his fangs a pale pink. It's *my blood* that splatters against my face as he opens his mouth to taunt me.

Even though tears burn behind my eyes, I refuse to cry. But I do scream. The moment the vampire wraps his dirt-caked, bloodstained hand around my neck, I bellow. I scratch at his fingers with my one good hand, but it's no use. He's too strong.

Without hesitation behind his shining crimson eyes, he clenches his fist, crushing my throat.

Mamá screams my name as I gasp for air. In heavy, uneven breaths, I ask the elements to heal me. But they refuse me, for I'm not strong enough to wield all five at once.

I scratch at the vampire straddling me, but he simply smiles.

My eyelids grow heavier with each passing second as I struggle to breathe. I'm only moments away from certain death, and as my soul begins to slip into the afterlife, I panic.

My killer must grow tired of watching me struggle to hold on to life, because he stands and joins the rest of the vampires in their assault against my coven, leaving me with nothing but the welcoming darkness.

"Look at me," someone says. "Focus."

His voice is smooth and echoes in my head. His words twist around me, lifting me to him, to this world of agony. Torn away from my blissful demise, I open my eyes.

His crimson-red irises stare back at me, and I nearly choke on my tongue.

This vampire is so close—*too close.*

He kneels on the ground over me, holding my bruised body against his. My head, too heavy for me to lift, is supported by his other hand. Only inches away from my face, his breath is hot on my cheek, his hand cool on my back. I don't recognize him.

Tearing my watery gaze from his, I search for Mamá in the midst of a war.

Help!

I shout the words in my head, but of course, no one hears me. My coven mates are fighting their own battles. A vampire lunges to attack a water witch, and she falls to the ground, screaming, but another vampire appears by her side.

He withdraws a dagger from his belt and slams it into the other vampire's chest. As dust scatters all around them, he yells for the witch to run, to save herself.

What's happening?

The realization sinks in that some vampires are fighting on the side of the witches to help save my coven.

Who are these vampires? How is this possible?

Unfortunately, our saviors can't help everyone. Bodies are scattered across the sacred ground of our ritual space.

Witches.

Vampires.

Their fragmented bits and broken bodies look eerily identical in the moonlit patches. Blood stains what was once lush green grass. But whose blood is it? This red wave of defeat mixes together seamlessly without a care about its source or the feuding creatures who contributed.

The witches call upon their elements. Air slices through flesh, piercing vampire hearts, as the witches try to save themselves. Fire witches aid those who are less fortunate, like those who control water or even earth.

My people are badly wounded, and they need my help.

Staring once again into his eyes, the world melts away. I choke on my breath, and my sputtering heart makes it hard to focus.

I will not fail my coven. I will not leave them unprotected.

The pain begins to subside, and I know death is my saving grace. In a last desperate attempt to survive, I beg for salvation.

Save me. I mouth the words, knowing there is only one way he knows how.

My grip on life is weakening, and in my most desperate of times, I see my reprieve in his eyes. As life slips through my grasp, I panic. I will offer anything to survive this attack, to save my coven—even if the only thing I have to offer is my mortality.

I whimper and scratch at his body with my one good hand, and his fangs lengthen into two bloodthirsty points.

His crimson irises take on an eerie glow as he allows the demon within him to surface. With a slight whimper, I turn my head, exposing my brutalized neck.

I watch the world around me, struggling to focus on anything but what's about to happen, what I'm about to give up.

The remaining members of my coven fight to control their magic against the vampires who wish us harm—against what I am to become.

These newcomers look different than the murderous eyes around us. The animals who attacked us and still surround us are just that: animals. Their dirty, bloodstained bodies contain the souls of fiends.

I gasp as my neck is pierced one final time. I dig my nails into his arms, marking him like he marks me. It's over before I truly realize it's even begun.

He glances down at me, a steady stream of my blood slides down his chin, and my stomach twists into knots. I must grimace, because he frowns at me. My vision blurs from tears, and I blink to push them away.

"Are you sure?" he asks, and I nod.

He tips my head back, opening my mouth. He presses his body against me, raising a hand. He bites into his wrist and offers it to me. A metallic-tasting substance drips into my open mouth. His essence, his power, soars through me, healing wounds as it floods each crevice of my broken body.

Wrapped in a warm blanket of bliss, I slide my hand up his strong, muscular arms, tangling my fingers in his hair.

I hold on to him, drinking as though he is my only source of water in the midst of a desert.

Briefly, I forget the world around us. I forget about the war and my hatred for vampires. I even forget about my impending death.

There is only him.

There is only me.

There is only blood.

SIX

You need to wake, Ava.

Mamá's voice echoes in my mind. She stands before me, slowly backing away. The light follows her exit. I thrash and plead for an escape, fearing the inevitable darkness she will leave behind. The air is hazy and thick, and I struggle to breathe, to stay awake.

"Mamá?" I say, unable to hide the fear in my voice. My words echo all around me. I am trapped in my own skin. I see nothing but a void, and time stands still. I can feel the darkness of eternity closing in, making its new home within me.

I run toward her, grabbing on to her flowing sheer white gown. My fingers fall numb, unable to grip as the fabric slips through.

"Please don't leave me," I beg.

The shadow moves closer, circling me. I whip around, lashing back and forth, but it has already ensnared me. Her silhouette slowly begins to fade. The darkness is consuming her, just as it will consume me too. It moves closer with each step I take back.

My lungs fill with the misty air, and I fall to my knees, hacking. I am drowning—drowning without being submerged in water. The darkness, the air, the haze, it consumes me, stealing away my breath, forcing me to my knees, to beg for life.

Ava, she says, and I look up, my chest heaving. *Wake up.*

Mamá speaks to me, yet her lips never move. I reach out, but my limb falls numb, hitting the ground in a thump. I slump over, unable to hold my own weight. My breath comes in short bursts.

I'm dying.

I know this to be true. The empty void that surrounds me and the darkness closing in is penance for asking the vampire to save my soul. Oh, the irony of asking a damned creature to save me . . . I am forced to spend an eternity in solitude with nothing but my thoughts and the lingering regret.

If the witches fear nothing else, they fear the vampire species.

And I asked to become one of them.

I look up at Mamá as I accept my fate. She gives me one final glance before fading into the darkness.

❖

"Leave immediately." Mamá's voice squeaks under her threatening tone.

Darkness still surrounds me, but the familiar scent of home creeps in. I inhale deeply and find comfort in the sage smoke that wafts through the air.

"She'll awaken soon," a man says. I recognize his voice. He's not a witch from our coven; he's the vampire who agreed to snap my mortal coil from its earthly existence.

Something within me twists into knots. I don't feel good about this, about this man.

I fight to wake, to stand, to scream, to do *something*, *anything at all*. But I can't. I'm trapped inside my body, an unyielding shell that withstands my internal protests.

"And when she does, we'll send her on her way. You're *all* not welcome here," Mamá says.

My heart sinks into the pit of my stomach, which grumbles from hunger.

"Just relax. We won't bite," someone else says. I don't recognize his voice, but I'm sure he came with the other vampire.

The vampire's joke makes me cringe. I'm sure he thinks it's funny, but all I can think about is sinking my stake into his chest. The metal would slide through him with such ease, like a knife through warm butter.

My heart beats faster; the stammering noise makes it hard to concentrate on the conversation happening around me.

I focus all my energy into moving my hand. It's nearly impossible . . . until it isn't. My arm twitches. My eyelids shoot open. My back arches as my muscles spasm, and I let out an uncontrollable screech that nearly shakes the house to its foundation.

I am no longer in control of my body as it transitions from mortal to immortal, from creature of the day to beast of the night.

My muscles tense, and I flop around like a fish in search of water. My chest constricts, nearly caving in, and I release a loud bellow. My voice doesn't sound like my own.

I feel . . . different. Lighter. Stronger.

The pain is excruciating, and I'm unsure how long I'll be on this limbo plane. I sense my body moving, but I can't stop it. It moves on its own, and I wonder if I'll be like this forever. Am I cursed to forever feel unlike myself?

But then everything stops. The pain diminishes, my

muscles loosen, and my mind clears. It's an ecstatic sensation unlike anything I've ever felt.

The door to my bedroom flings open, and I find myself off my bed and backing away from him until I'm flush against the wall. His crimson irises burn brightly. This is the man who was supposed to be my savior. I don't know him. In fact, prior to tonight, I've never seen him before. I don't know why he was in Darkhaven when the other vampires attacked us, and I don't know why he tried to help us. Vampires aren't supposed to be friendly with witches.

Slowly, he walks toward me. Time slows as he approaches. Palms against the cool walls, I dig my nails into the drywall and growl. He takes another step closer, his scent wafting toward me. He smells like cinnamon and blood. It's an oddly delicious mixture that makes my stomach ache.

Several figures enter behind the vampire, crowding me, cornering me. A drip of drool dribbles down my chin as the scent from my bloodstained clothes reaches my nose. The air is thick and heavy as we sit in silence. The scent of fresh meat mingles in the air, causing my stomach to grumble.

"You should leave," the vampire says. He turns to face the witches, who are also on guard. This brief moment, when his eyes are turned away from me, is all I need.

Fangs exposed, I lunge forward. I reach for the vampire's throat, clawing my way through flesh. He's strong, maybe too strong, so I smack my fists against him until he's flying across the room and slamming into the group behind him.

I set my sights on the next closest thing: a witch. And not just any witch. Mamá.

I know it's wrong. I don't want to hurt her, but I can't stop. I'm too hungry. My belly feels like an acidic pit, and it's bubbling over. It must be sated.

"Stop, *mija*!" Mamá cries, but her plea falls upon deaf ears.

Before I can reach her, I am thrown backward into the far wall. Framed pictures shatter against the floor beside me. I jump to my feet and am met by another witch. Her stretched-out arm is all that separates the distance between us. She draws her index and middle fingers out just as a warrior would draw a sword upon her enemies.

I smile and inhale deeply, licking my lips. She smells like herbs. She smells like *food*.

"Please don't make me hurt you, Ava," the witch says. "Listen to my voice. You can fight this."

She doesn't know that I can't. She doesn't understand—none of them do. I don't *want* to hurt them, but the pungent bite of hunger is in my gut. It stings at my innards until there's nothing but gooey remnants of my past good intentions.

Furrowing my brow, I release another powerful growl, and the monster within me leaves me with no other options. I take a step forward, and the witch yanks her fingers into her palm before instantly throwing them out again.

Her powerful air magic pins me to the wall, but I don't have to withstand her fury for long.

My vampire savior steps before me, grabbing my arms and slamming my body against the wall. Angry, confused, and starving, I stare at his neck. He's close—*too close*. A thick, protruding vein is only one bite away. My fangs lengthen instinctively, and my muscles loosen beneath his grasp. I no longer wish to escape him.

"Control yourself," he orders. "You are the master of your hunger, not the other way around."

He relaxes his grip, and I fall against him. I wrap my arms

around him and relish in the feeling of his soft tresses against my palms. I bury my nose into the crevice of his neck, inhaling slowly, deeply. His scent overwhelms me. There's something familiar about it, about him.

"Jasik..." someone whispers.

The cautionary voice breaks my trance. I focus on the vampire's sputtering heart as I wrap my arms tighter around him. Blood pumps faster in his veins, teasing me, testing me. He groans as I place the tips of my fangs against the soft skin of his neck. I don't apply force because I want him to beg me to bite him. And I'm confident he will.

"Fight it," the concerned bystander shouts.

"We'll feed soon," another says.

Irritated, I glance toward the speakers. Three vampires, mere feet from us, stand strong beside the witches, beside their mortal enemies. Everyone's attention is on me and on the vampire in my arms.

He tries to pull away, but I yank him back to me. He is powerless beneath my grip; the control I have over his life is euphoric. I glance up, meeting his gaze. We're breathing the same air. We're so close, our lips nearly touch, and my world spins.

In one swift motion, he twists my arms, releasing himself from my grasp, spinning free until he can take several steps backward.

I'm spun completely around until I'm facing the opposite direction. It's an uneasy feeling to have my back turned to everyone in the room. Something in me sparks. A warning. The predator within me doesn't like to be in this vulnerable state.

My gaze settles on the full-length body mirror in the corner of my bedroom. I'm staring at my reflection so intensely,

I don't realize the vampire is behind me, and even when I notice him there, I don't care that he's too close for comfort. I only care about the girl in the mirror.

"You mustn't lose yourself to the hunger," he whispers, his breath hot against my ear.

A pang of desire creeps through my body as I admire his closeness. I push it down, disgusted.

"Look at yourself," he says, his breath tickling my earlobe.

My brown hair hangs raggedly at my shoulders. My frame is toned, defined, and my complexion is clear, pale. My eyes are no longer their natural plain dark-brown color. They are bright crimson, almost neon in shade. My entire appearance, from my disheveled look to my glowing eyes, is jarring.

I eliminate the space between the mirror and me and place my palms and the tip of my nose against the glass. The girl who stands before me is no one I recognize. Through lacy puffs of exhalations, her figure disappears and reappears as my breath clouds my reflection in the mirror before I turn to scan my bedroom.

A cluttered desk sits in the corner. Yellowed photos and rusted medals from my former life sit atop the chipped wood table. It feels like a lifetime has passed since I was that girl.

Bundles of crumpled clothes are piled on the floor, and a sheetless bed is positioned between two big windows. Everything about this room feels familiar yet foreign. It's as if I suddenly don't belong in the place I've always called home.

Bile creeps its way into my throat, and I swallow it down. I remember everything from the night before—asking the vampire to save my life by changing me, the fight, the fear. I remember death.

"Were there casualties?" I ask Mamá, ignoring the

overwhelming sensation to rip out her throat. My stomach is burning, so I squeeze my palms shut and focus on the pain in my hands rather than the one in my gut.

"Yes, and they were severe," she replies slowly. Her gaze trails down my frame. She looks...distant, unsure...afraid. She's afraid of me, her daughter. She's afraid of what I've become. It pains me to see her hesitant even to speak to me, her own flesh and blood.

Blood.

My breath catches at the sound of blood moving through her veins. The rushing sensation is all around me, enveloping me. I lick my lips and close my eyes.

Breathe. Just breathe. I focus on each inhalation. One in. One out.

Someone grabs on to my hand, interlocking fingers with my own. Smiling, I open my eyes, expecting to see Mamá beside me, trusting me that I would never hurt her or our coven members.

But he is there. The vampire looks down at me. His lips form a hard line in a fake, forced smile. I rip my hand from his grasp before quickly bringing it up again and thrusting, landing a blow squarely in the center of his chest. He flies through the air with the ease of a feather blowing in the breeze.

"Don't touch me!" I shout. The vampire has already landed against the far wall. He's standing and dusting off his shirt. He moves quickly, effortlessly, like he's been around long enough to perfect his vampire reflexes.

"Ava, I promise I'm not going to hurt you."

His words seem sincere. Every fiber of my being wants to trust him, to take his hand, to believe I will be okay. But I know the truth. I'm a vampire now. I'm *never* going to be okay.

My coven will disown me. Even if there were such a thing as a tame vampire, they would never allow me to stay here with them. They wouldn't risk it.

I failed them. How could I give up so easily? I failed my coven the moment I practically begged to be turned into a vampire. Now I'm going to be hunted by those I've spent my life protecting.

"You'll feel better once you've fed," he says. "Your mind will clear."

He speaks to me as if we are the only two in the room. His eyes, like his tone, are sincere. I don't understand why, but I believe he cares for me. He wants to protect me. Somehow, we've bonded in a way I'll probably never accept or understand.

I think back to my hours of preparation for the ritual. Deep down, I knew the vampires were there, watching, waiting in the woods. I *felt* them. They were close enough to make me feel physically ill. I blamed those sensations on nerves, but in reality, spirit was warning me of my impending doom.

"Mamá . . . please don't make me leave," I whisper.

"Ava López," she responds, her voice quivering and tears forming behind her eyes.

My heart nearly stops as I wait for her to pass down sentencing. Regardless of whether or not a witch chooses to become a vampire, the sentence is always the same: death.

With everyone's eyes on me, I stand tall to show onlookers that I'm strong enough to accept my sentence. After all, I would have died to protect my coven. How is this any different?

"I hereby relinquish your duty to this coven. You are no longer a member, nor are you family. Due to your previous status in this coven, I will grant you two minutes. Say your goodbyes, gather your things, and leave."

The seconds tick by as I process her words. The strokes of the hallway grandfather clock echo all around me.

Tears burn as I nod in response. But she is not sentencing me to death, and this will cost her later. When our high priestess discovers Mamá's weakness, she will pay for her leniency.

"Should you not be gone within two minutes, we will release our full power on you."

She stops speaking, and I wait for her to finish. But she says nothing. She can't actually say the words aloud. She can't say that she will *kill* me, her only daughter.

The witches around her tense. Are they worried she will order them to kill me? Do they want to? I'm no longer family.

I'm a threat.

I shuffle into my bathroom and close the door behind me. Neatly folded clothes are piled atop the counter, placed there hours ago by me so I could easily change out of my ritual gown. I dress quickly, stripping off the cloak and dressing in my usual black combat attire. I slide on my boots and grab my toiletries.

When I walk back into my room, the witches and vampires are still standing in the same spot. No one has moved, and everyone is clearly uneasy about the situation. I imagine they're all counting the seconds.

I say nothing as I quickly fill my bag with enough clothes to last me several days and then stop at my dresser, tossing the sleek black box that contains my stake into the bag. I open my jewelry box and remove the necklace Papá gave me, dropping it into my bag without touching the metal cross. I may not be able to wear it anymore, but I still want it with me.

I glance around the room. My pictures are a shattered mess on the floor. My books from online classes are in stacks on my desk. Dirty and clean clothes are in piles on the floor.

What else should I take?

"Ava, we must leave," my vampire savior says.

I sniffle as I walk over to my photo album. Quickly, I shove it into my bag. I zip it closed and throw the strap over my shoulder. Everything I have left in my life is tucked away in a medium-sized travel bag I bought from a secondhand tote store.

My two minutes are nearly up, and Mamá is likely paranoid I'll miss my deadline. But I won't. I'd never force her to choose between me and her duty as the high priestess's daughter-in-law.

I scan my room one final time, my gaze landing on each witch in a silent goodbye. Most won't even meet my gaze. When my eyes land on a familiar set of crimson irises, I trudge closer to him. In a room full of enemies, this vampire might be my only ally. His eyes beckon to me as if he's silently asking me to trust him.

I rush from my room and take the stairs two at a time. My deadline expires the moment I pass the threshold and greet the outside air, its cool breeze refreshing against my skin. I beg for it to blow away the fear, doubt, and pain that cloud my mind.

With only the slightest inhalation, I am discovering new scents. From flowers to meat and rust to salt, I smell the world as if life is sprawled on a platter before me. But it's so much more than that. I can *feel* it. Life that drives nature enters my senses and flows through me. It's as if I can tap into Mother Earth's energy and harness it as my own.

"You show an impressive level of control I've yet to see in a newborn," the vampire says.

I don't respond. I'm not exactly thankful that I excel at being a vampire.

"I'm Jasik," he continues.

Again, I don't know what to say. He knows my name. Maybe I should tell him I don't want to go with him, but where else can I go? I don't have any other options. If I stay behind, the witches will kill me. If I go out alone, I might hurt someone. Whether I like it or not, I need the vampires. I need them to teach me how to be one, how to control my urges. If I can prove to my coven that I'm not a danger to them . . . I could become the ultimate hunter. They might accept me then.

"We need to get back. The sun's rising soon," another vampire says.

He glances at me, jaw clenched. I feel vulnerable under his stare. He doesn't look at me with wonder or curiosity or lust. He looks at me with . . . fear. Or is it disgust and hatred I see behind his thick lashes? Quickly, he turns away to join the other two vampires.

It feels odd to be among them. I feel vulnerable yet safe. My innate hatred for them is tinged with curiosity.

"That's Malik, my brother."

I glance back at my house. My gaze lingers on my bedroom window. Mamá stands beside the curtain, watching me before quickly stepping out of view. I want to call out to her and beg her to let me stay, but leaving is my only option. My coven will never be safe with me around unless I learn to control my hunger.

I kick a stone with my foot, watching it bounce against the concrete, stopping once it reaches a patch of grass. The pavement's vibrations rattle through my body as the stone glides against it.

Glancing up from the ground, I watch as two teenagers approach us. The boy has his arm around the back of the girl's neck, pulling her close to him. She smiles as he does this, probably enjoying the safety he provides—not realizing that there are monsters in this world far stronger than he could ever imagine.

I examine his physique as a scientist would in a laboratory. His arms and chest are tightly bound by his T-shirt. Thin white lines dance across his pale skin. Stretch marks. The closer we become, the more I see. Goose bumps cover his skin; fine hairs stand on end. The air was cool during the ritual, but I don't feel chilly now. I feel the breeze but not the cold.

They are just a few feet in front of us now. His shirt seems to become tighter and tighter the closer we get. I wonder if he takes steroids.

Time slows as they pass. The wind picks up, blowing their scent into my open and willing nostrils. I lick my lips, my tongue sticking to dry parts of skin.

Shutting my eyes, I swallow hard as my throat begins to close. Its dryness is painful, scratchy. When I open my eyes again, my fangs are exposed, and I am just steps behind the humans. I don't know how I got there, and I don't care. An arm's length is all that separates them from death, from *me*. Just before I can leap at them from behind, I am yanked backward.

"Remember who you are." Jasik's voice is stern, controlling. I am shocked that he even cares. Vampires are murderers. Why would he stop me?

Looking up, I meet his eyes. I don't understand why he stopped me, but I'm thankful he did. Remembering who I am is becoming more and more difficult as the night progresses. Jasik's proximity feels oddly intimate, making my skin burn. My fangs retract, and I pull away from my captor, horrified at my newfound hunger.

I shake my head and wrap my body in my arms. In that moment, I didn't care if I took that teenager's life. I lost control. I wanted to kill—I was *ready* to kill. But I didn't feel like a killer. I just felt *hungry*.

I drop my arms and resort to the only thing I know how to do in this new world: I run.

SEVEN

Someone is calling after me, but his voice quickly grows faint. As I run down the street toward the unoccupied woods that surround Darkhaven, the trees begin to blur at my sides, yet the world remains clear before me. As my feet pound against the hard-packed ground, my legs never grow tired. Wary of my strength, I come to an abrupt stop and fall to my knees.

"What have I become?" I say aloud, burying my face in my palms.

"Ava?" a voice says. Footsteps approach from behind.

I jump to my feet and spin around. The vampires approach me with caution.

We are in a small clearing. The forest that surrounds Darkhaven often protects me from prying eyes while patrolling. I find comfort in seclusion. I know these woods in the dead of night. I know the trails to find home, the berries that grow in the bushes, and the hidden cemetery where my coven buries our loved ones. These woods are part of my life, my family. I'm sickened to think of vampires using the earth as their hunting ground.

"Everything will be okay. You're reckless because of the hunger," Jasik says.

His words are soothing. I am angry, confused, but as soon

as he speaks, I calm. His reassurance is all it takes to make me feel some semblance of peace, even when only moments before a storm raged within me. The thought of him having power over me leaves me sick. I refuse to believe he has such sway over my irrational emotions.

I shake my head. "How can I be okay? I don't even know what I am anymore."

"We'll find something to eat," he says.

His words and confidence annoy me. How is it that the undead thing before me is so optimistic?

"I'll go with Hikari and Jeremiah. You'll be all right?" Malik asks.

Jasik nods without breaking eye contact, and when the others finally leave, I blurt out the question I've been itching to ask.

"Why did you save me?" The question sounds stupid as it leaves my lips. His answer should be simple, right? He saved me because I begged him to. But I'm not so sure that was his only motive. I'm sure it's a complicated answer, because there are too many parts. And it isn't my only question for him.

Why were they there the night of our ritual?

Did they know what was going to happen that night?

How did they rescue my coven in time?

Why did they even try to save us?

Was this the first time they were so close to my home?

I have so many questions, and I don't know where to begin.

"Why did you help us?" I press on.

"We were hunting the rogue vampires that attacked your coven. We wouldn't have stepped in, but we could see you were outnumbered. You were already injured. The scent of blood was heavy in the air. If the rogue vampires weren't stopped, they would have gone on to decimate the village. We had to stop them."

As he speaks, his eyes grow distant. I can't understand why talking about the other vampires affects him as much as it seems to, and I hate that I even care that it bothers him. I don't understand the connection that now ties us together.

But more so, I hate me. I hate my decision to become a vampire. I hate my fear of dying. I hate that I didn't trust my coven to save me after the attack. I should have trusted in our combined power to heal my wounds.

Most importantly, I hate that I don't really hate the vampire before me. I'm not afraid of him because, deep down, I know he doesn't want to hurt me. If he did, he wouldn't have saved me. I want to despise everything he is, but I can't. Has transitioning into a vampire changed more of me than just the superficial stuff?

"If we arrived even one minute later, we wouldn't have been able to save you," he whispers.

"Do you make a habit of hunting your own kind?" I ask. It's a serious question, but I can't help my mocking tone.

"Yes," he says plainly.

I arch a brow in response and wait for him to continue.

"Just like any species, we have some…problems. Vampires who indulge in a risky lifestyle must be eliminated. We fear exposure as much as witches do."

"I guess I never thought of that. Every time I've patrolled, I've encountered vampires who were hunting. I've never met a vampire like you."

"Well, you should know that I do feed. All vampires do. But I don't make a point to murder countless humans in the name of boredom. We have rules in place for purely selfish reasons. Vampires can never outnumber humans. And our survival depends on their ignorance."

I nod. "I suppose it does."

"Witches are no different. Look what happened the last time humans thought they encountered witches. Your ancestors are still suffering from those trials."

I realize now I've never actually thanked him for saving us. He might have been forced to turn me, but because he and his friends helped us, the other witches are okay. I fear that's a debt I can never repay.

"Listen, this isn't easy for me, but—" I exhale sharply. "Thank you for saving my family and for killing the rogue vampires."

He clears his throat. "We didn't exactly eliminate the threat."

"What do you mean? You killed them all, didn't you?"

A gnawing in the pit of my gut is telling me I missed something; it's an instinctual predatory reaction I honed the moment I witnessed the death of my father. I learned to kill or be killed.

I think back to the fight. I passed out before it ended. I saw some vampires die, but what happened to the vampire who bit me, the one who threatened Liv and me in the cemetery the night before the ritual? Is he dead? Will he come back? Mamá doesn't know the whole story. She won't be prepared for another battle.

"We killed all but a few," Jasik says, confirming my suspicions.

My world comes crashing down as the realization hits me hard. The vampire who stole my life from me—the vampire who forced me to become what I am—still walks, still lives, still breathes. Jasik doesn't need to confirm this. Somehow, I just *know* he's still out there somewhere.

Anger boils within me as an acidic slop rises in my chest. I force it down in a quick gulp. The thought makes me sick, furious. He should be dead. Everyone who had any part in the attack should have perished beside the fallen members of my coven. I will make him pay for what he did. There will be a time for vengeance, but unfortunately, that time isn't now.

I relax my body, shaking away the anger, the nerves, the tightness. I close my eyes and focus on my breath. Inhaling through my nose, exhaling through my mouth, I picture the world around me.

The moon has reached its peak, and as it slowly sets, the sun will soon rise. I focus on her, on Mother Nature, on her power—the power that is nestled in all her children.

As a spirit user, I had a small affinity for all magic because spirit is everywhere, in everything, but I never perfected my skill of using the other elements for long periods of time. I was good for a blast of fire here and there, but that was about it. I reach within myself, tugging the new part of me that contains my heightened vampire senses and pull it toward the part of me that holds on to my past. Maybe, with enough practice, I can blend the two worlds and finally feel safe and strong in my new skin. I need to believe that I didn't *turn*. I *transitioned* into a better, more powerful version of myself.

Sticks crack in the distance, jolting us out of our conversational trance. Jasik spins around, his hand easily maneuvering his blade from its sheath. He steps before me, protectively blocking my body with his own. I step beside him in a defiant move to show him I don't need his protection. I can protect myself.

75

Malik stands only a few feet from us, jaw clenched, face hard. His characteristics mirror many of his brother's features, but it's clear Malik is older. He has age, a wisdom about him that clearly showcases his no-nonsense attitude.

"We found something," Malik says.

Jasik nods, slides his weapon back into place, and walks toward his brother.

Its scent reaches my nostrils before its dying whimpers reach my ears. Its blood coats the air, making it heavy like the air after a rainfall. I've never desired something so much in my life; knowing how close it is to me now, it's almost too difficult to breathe.

The vampires lead me to a dying wolf. Its matted gray-and-white hair is stained with blood.

As the smell hits me, a wave of hunger rocks my insides. My stomach lurches as if I haven't eaten in days, and my tongue dries. My muscles tighten as I rub my dry tongue over my lips. I begin to shake, and as each second passes, it becomes more difficult to control the urge to feed.

My fangs lengthen as I release a small growl. I am no longer in control. The part of me that rises to the surface is more terrifying than the vampires that surround me. I pounce on the wolf. I give in to the need, to the darkness, to everything I prayed I would never become.

Digging my fangs into its body, I drink hard and long. Expecting it to taste no differently than rusty water, I am surprised when the thick substance coating my tongue tastes refreshing. It is sweet with a hint of bitterness, but most importantly, it is delicious. My muscles feel stronger, my senses more alert. I scrunch the wolf's fur in my hands, pushing my face deeper into its carcass; it ceases to struggle and whimper as it takes its last breath.

Something in the brush moves toward me, and I dart my gaze to meet a pack of wolves emerging from the tree line. A large wolf steps forward and releases a loud growl. It's challenging me. I have killed a member of its pack, and it is the alpha's duty to protect its remaining members. But I refuse to forfeit my meal.

I jump to my feet and spring before it. With my foot, I push the carcass farther behind me. I pull my lips up, further exposing my fangs. Streams of blood trickle down my chin, and I release a growl. The alpha meets my gaze and holds it, but I refuse to look away. He challenges me for only a second before the pack begins to slowly back away.

Waiting until they are no longer audible, I relax my strained muscles and sit down beside the dead wolf. I finish the final slurps and lick the drips of blood from my chin.

I've forgotten who I am. I've killed a living creature, a child of Mother Nature. As a witch, I was raised to love all living things. We never abstained from eating meat, but my coven respected nature and lived peacefully among animals. We learned to give our livestock a peaceful life—and death. What I've done is disgraceful.

I stand, looking down at my hands. Chunks of gray matted fur coat my fingers. Holding my hands up for the others to see, I begin to shake, and I look at Jasik. I whimper, my breath coming in short bursts. I don't know why I look to him, but I need someone, anyone, to tell me what I just did was okay.

He takes the few steps that separate us and wraps his arms around me, digging the fingers of his free hand into my hair. He rests his chin atop my head.

"I promise it will become easier with time."

I ignore his words. I killed something, and worst of all, I enjoyed it. I want him to tell me it is okay. I want him to make me forget. But I'm not ready to hear that it will become *easier* to kill an animal or to feed from a person.

Pulling away from him, I wipe my hands on a patch of grass, desperately trying to remove all evidence of my despicable actions. I sniffle as I walk toward the vampires, not looking back at the mess I've left behind.

EIGHT

I'm running farther away from the life I don't want to leave and closer to the life I never wanted.

Vampires are all around me. Two lead the way, and a third trails behind. I can feel Malik's eyes on me, silently judging every decision I make. I can sense he feels strongly about me, but I'm not quite sure what it is he feels. I'm not even sure if *he* knows how he feels about this situation. After all, how often does Jasik turn humans into vampires? Does he make this regular practice? Or has he just risked his neck to save mine?

Jasik is beside me. Only a few feet of space separate us. His presence is suffocating. Something about him is frustratingly alluring. The moment I fed from him, we bonded. I don't need him to confirm that what he did for me was some sort of eternal agreement between us. The unspoken contract is like a noose around my neck. I'm not sure how to shake myself from his grasp, but I'm certain I'll find a way. Thanks to him, I have a lot of time to plan my escape.

We run, and I focus on my surroundings, trying to ignore the vampires. I don't know what's more unsettling—their proximity or how easy it is for me to forget about them. The only other times I've been this close to vampires, I was fighting for my life. As much as I don't want to find my sanctuary with them, I don't have any other options. I can't allow my blood lust to get the best of me.

My overnight bag hangs heavily across my chest. The strap smacks against my torso as I run, the weight of what little remains in my life almost unbearable. I carry it with little effort, even though I know what's inside—all the things I can no longer have.

A cross necklace that will burn my skin.

A silver stake doused in witch magic I can no longer access.

A photo album memorializing times in my life I can no longer cherish now that I've been forsaken.

Aside from those three items, all that's left are the material things we all need to survive: a few outfits and toiletry items.

That's it.

That's my life.

A sudden thought comes to me. *I never said goodbye to Liv.* I never even checked on her. Everything happened so fast. She was gone when I woke, and I just assumed I would talk to her after the full moon ritual. It's just now occurring to me that last night could have been our final goodbye.

What will she think when the rumors spread? She'll hear about the attack and that I willingly changed and left with the vampires. Like the rest, she'll hate me.

I swallow the knot that forms in my throat and push on. I have to stay strong. My stomach still aches from hunger, and I'm beginning to shake. I wasted too much of the wolf's offering. If I don't feed soon . . .

A shiver rushes through my body at the thought of feeding, and it both disgusts and excites me. Jasik offers a curious sideways glance. I shake my head, silently telling him not to ask, to let it go. I'm sure he knows the symptoms of starvation, and I need to feed if I want to survive the transition.

And I do, right? I *want* to survive, to become a vampire, to be reunited with my family.

I don't know where we're going, but Jasik said their vampire nest is within Darkhaven's city limits. Oddly, I find comfort in knowing I'll still be close to home, but in the same breath, I'm uneasy from the realization that vampires have been calling Darkhaven home all this time. Clearly my patrols weren't as effective as I thought they were.

The vampires leading our way come to a sudden stop. The surrounding woods that encircle our small village clear, and I come face-to-face with a timeless Victorian-style manor three stories tall, with startling overhangs, sharp edges, and stained-glass windows. The wraparound porch is vacant save for two stone gargoyles on either side of the front walk. The stairs lead to French-style double doors crafted from wood stained so dark they almost match the house's exterior color. The dark sky is brightening in the distance as the sun begins to rise, and I find myself focusing on the manor's exterior paint color. Is it dark green? Or perhaps blue. Or maybe it's a mix, a dark grayish blue.

The rooftop comes to several different points, all abrupt in composition, with a subtle yet striking weather vane as the front focal point. The typical rooster has been replaced with a prominent spear, a death dagger that pierces the sky. I'm not sure if the distraction is intentional, but the feature steals my attention for several breaths. In fact, the entire property is breathtaking. It's dark and dank, yet the antiquity of it is beautiful. It's my new home.

It's not quite what I was expecting when I think *vampire nest*. I'll admit, I didn't give much thought to the living arrangements when I trusted the vampires to take me to their nest, but considering it now, I'm not sure why I didn't assume I'd be spending my days holed up in a cave or something. I mean, who would have thought vampires live a life of luxury?

The house is surrounded by a short black wrought-iron fence. Each point of the daggers encompassing the manor ends in two sharp slabs of metal that form tiny crosses. My gaze trails the fence as I cross the threshold into their world. I reach for the metal, and just as my fingertips graze the cross, I'm stopped. Jasik's hand firmly grasps my own. He doesn't speak until we make eye contact.

"Don't," he says simply.

I nod in understanding and pull away from him. Only a second ago, I was overwhelmed by my new home, but now, all I can think about is the fact that I can no longer touch crosses, and there's one cross I'd very much like to wear and never remove. It's all I have left of Papá. I sigh and continue trudging toward the front door while scanning my surroundings.

The grass is overgrown in all the places that border the house and fence, and it's dead in all the places the trees block sunlight. Weeds run rampant through the yard, leaving splashes of vibrant yellow flowers scattered among the grass. The sight is jarring, so I focus on the cobblestone path that leads to the front door.

"How have I never noticed this house before?" I say.

"No one ventures this far into the woods," Jasik replies.

He stops my racing thoughts, which run on a never-ending loop. I was so consumed by the property, I didn't realize I'd spoken aloud. His response makes sense. This property is at the far edge of Darkhaven, which is surrounded by forest on three sides and the sea on another. It's an old village full of tenth-generation families. The settlers who formed it stayed—and so did their descendants. The architecture mirrors that of seventeenth-century Salem, not nineteenth-century England. That could only mean one thing: vampires settled here long after witches. How did they find our little village and manage to build such a prominent residence under our very noses?

"Thank the Goddess for that, right?" I say sarcastically.

Jasik arches a brow.

"We wouldn't want humans venturing too close to home," I say pointedly.

"I fear your impression of vampires is ... distasteful," he says.

I shrug. "I speak from experience."

"You speak based solely on what you were taught to believe."

"Are you suggesting my family has been dishonest?" I stop abruptly and turn to face him, crossing my arms over my chest.

"It would appear that way."

I'm annoyed by his confidence, even though a twinge of regret builds within me. How can I be angry with him when he's shown me a much softer side than I'm used to? He protected us and chose to fight by our side when the other vampires attacked. He saved my life. He stopped me from killing those humans.

He's right. The witches have never told me there were vampires out there who wanted to coexist. Knowing what I know now, would I have stopped my patrols? Would I have hunted all those vampires? Would my coven have disowned me years ago if I believed we could live among vampires in peace?

Before I can respond to his accusation, the front doors to

the manor swing open, smacking against the walls on either side. One figure stands prominently in the doorway. She stares at me with an intensity that makes my skin crawl and heart burn. I can practically *feel* her anger.

Seconds tick by, and I take this time to assess the threat. She's tall, thin. Her shiny black hair is sleek and brushed back, and the ends hang raggedly above her shoulders. Her long-sleeved black dress is lacy and sheer, revealing the delicate curves of her small frame. Everything about her makes her look weak, but I'm certain she's not. It's a disguise that hides the powerful monster within.

She moves swiftly toward me, almost as if she's floating. Of course, I know she's not. Vampires only fly in the movies.

In a flash, she's standing before me. She reaches forward and grasps my chin between her fingers, snapping my head upward so our eyes meet. She watches me carefully. I don't speak. I don't even try to pull away. I'm mesmerized by her beauty and the power that radiates from her. I'm fairly certain if I were to fight this woman, I would lose, even with my newfound enhanced vampire strength. After spending several agonizing seconds inspecting me, she releases my chin and turns to face Jasik.

"How could you?" she hisses. Her voice is firm and smooth. Even though she's not speaking to me, or even looking at me, I'm overwhelmed with the desire to explain my actions, to apologize and beg for forgiveness. Something about this woman doesn't sit right with me. I want to please her in ways I can't even explain.

"She was dying," Jasik says. He averts his gaze from hers.

"She's a *witch*!"

I don't miss how the word "witch" sits on her tongue. She

doesn't like my kind, and I'm not sure how her hatred is going to affect my prosperity. Will I even be welcomed here? And if I'm not, what am I going to do? There's nowhere I can go where I can learn to control my blood lust.

"Not anymore," Jasik says.

"Look at me," she orders, and he does—immediately. I wasn't sure before, but I know now. This woman is in charge. If I want to survive my transition, I need to be on her good side. I just hope she has one.

"I'm sorry," Jasik whispers. I sense his regret. It pierces my heart like a knife. I don't understand why it hurts so much that he regrets saving my life, but I can't shake the feeling.

"We have rules in place for a reason, Jasik."

He nods.

"And you are well aware of the consequences for breaking my rules."

"I am," he says.

I try to make eye contact, but he doesn't budge. He maintains complete control as this woman chastises him for saving my life. Anger builds within me. What was he supposed to do? Let me die? Is that what she'd prefer? Does she feel this way only because I'm a witch? Would she be this upset if he came home with a newly turned human?

She arches a brow, and a sly grin forms across her perfect face. The lingering moonlight dances across her dark skin. Her crimson irises glow in the night, and I can't help noticing the flash of joy in them. It's clear something has just occurred to her, and I fear for Jasik's life.

"Death becomes you." She speaks slowly, emphasizing each word. Her voice deepens, darkens, and her words twist around in my mind.

Death becomes you.

I pray this doesn't mean what I think it means.

Again, Jasik nods. Briefly, he breaks eye contact with this woman. He glances at me, and his eyes are filled with sorrow. But why? Is he afraid for himself or for me? Everything is happening too quickly. I don't know what to think or what to do. I can't turn to Jasik for answers because he's bound to this woman—probably in the same way I'm bound to him.

She unsheathes a dagger she had strapped to her waist. I didn't even notice she was armed. I was too busy romanticizing my vision of her. I was too busy hoping she wasn't going to kill Jasik . . . and then me.

She swipes the blade forward, and it slashes across Jasik's chest. A bloody line strikes his torso and bleeds into the fabric of his shirt. He doesn't even move. He doesn't cry out or fight back. He simply stands and waits.

But I can't.

I lunge forward, my legs having a mind of their own. I reach him in the few seconds it takes for the woman to jab her blade forward. Putting myself between Jasik and his attacker, I withstand the full force of her fury as inch after inch of metal sinks into my chest. It slides through my flesh, centimeters away from my heart. She roots it deeply inside me and lets it linger while we make eye contact.

Jasik gasps behind me. My body is pushed against his. He grabs on to my arms as I start to fall back from the force of my assault. His fingers dig into my flesh as he holds me upright.

The woman's smile fades, and then she quickly yanks the dagger from my chest. I shriek as it's removed. The sound of metal scraping against bone will forever play in my mind. The woman steps back and watches as my knees buckle.

I'm swooped into Jasik's arms before I can fall to the ground. My chest heaves, my pulse races, and my stomach burns. What little energy I have is desperately trying to heal my wound, and I fear if I don't feed, I will die. In my line of work, I never feared death, but now I'm clinging to life with everything I have.

"Do you see why I have my rules?" the woman says.

Jasik tears his gaze from mine to look at the woman. His forehead is creased from his concern, and I can see confusion and anger muddled in his crimson eyes.

He holds me close to him, and I lean in. His musky scent wafts all around me. I inhale deeply and let the scent of cinnamon consume me. He smells like Yule morning back at home. A thought occurs to me: I may never see another sabbat again.

"How could you?" he asks, seething. "You know she's sired to me!"

"The fact that she is bound to you is the reason why I went to such lengths to uncover her innate devotion. This is why I have rules. No one but me sires vampires in my own home. She will be a problem."

"You haven't even given her a chance," Jasik says.

"I don't need to. Why do you think I have this rule? You aren't the first vampire I've sired to bring home a pet."

"She isn't my *pet*. Rogue vampires attacked her coven while we were hunting. We couldn't risk allowing the witches to be turned by rogues. I prevented an even greater threat by turning her myself."

I focus on the truth in Jasik's words. He didn't save me because he cared or because he wants to coexist with witches. He saved me to claim my soul as his own—to prevent the other vampires from getting a witch first. The betrayal of knowing his truth hurts more than I care to admit. I thought I would be safe with him. I trusted him. I believed he actually cared about saving me, about helping my coven.

The woman doesn't speak as she considers his words.

"She won't become a problem, Amicia. Give her a chance," Jasik pleads.

Amicia. Clearly, she is the leader here. She makes the decisions, and my life is in her hands. Slowly, I'm beginning to heal. I can feel my flesh tethering together like a braided rope. Hopefully I'll only need a few more minutes of peace before I am well again.

Silence suspends around us like stagnant air as I wait for her to pass judgment on my soul. Will she offer me a chance? Or will Jasik's penance be taking my life?

"I will train her," someone says.

In the distance, Malik approaches us. Jasik's brother strides closer, his eyes on Amicia. Something passes between them. I'm not sure what it is, but I'm itching to find out.

"Do you think you can truly control a witch-turned-vampire?" Amicia asks him.

He nods. "If I can't, I'll take care of the situation for Jasik. Either way, the threat you fear will be eliminated."

I swallow hard, suppressing a gasp. I suppose I understand his earlier reservations. His brother risked his life to save me, even if it was for the greater good. If I had a sibling, I'd feel uneasy too. The last thing I'd want is to watch my sibling die at the hands of faulty leadership.

Before disappearing inside the dark manor, Amicia says, "If she makes me regret my leniency, *everyone* will be held accountable. I certainly hope she's worth your lives."

NINE

I'm dreaming.

I sit up, looking around. My head feels heavy, and the room is dark. As I stand and rise from the bed, it takes every bit of strength I can muster to walk just a few steps.

I look around the room, noticing the full-length corner mirror Mamá brought home for me last summer, the cracked wall that serves as a reminder of when I lost control and attacked my own coven, and the shattered picture frames that lie in piles on the floor. I lean down and glance at each photo.

The collage is of a beautiful girl. She smiles next to an older woman who closely resembles her. They hug each other as if nothing could tear apart their bond. In the next photo, the girl stands with an arched back, strong legs, and straight arms pointed toward the sky. She's wearing a metallic, sparkly leotard. In another picture, the girl is a child. She's standing beside a man who holds her close.

The girl is me, but at the same time, I'm not her anymore. In these photos, I look happy, as if life gave me everything I'd ever asked for. Our faces are the ultimate disguise for the turmoil that lies beneath. The girl in these pictures was used to hiding her inner demons; she had everyone fooled.

I set the photographs on the bedside table and walk around the bed, trailing my hand against the footboard. The door to the hallway is open, and clothes clutter the floor beside it. I left so abruptly I didn't have time to clean.

A scattering of Post-it Notes decorates the wall beside a desk. They're written in sloppy handwriting.

Write more poetry.

Help Liv with garden.

Clean closet.

A floorboard creaks behind me. I turn around, but no one is there.

The air is hazy as I walk through the room and toward the desk. On the desktop, there's a cluttering of homemade picture frames with superglued seashells stuck to the edges.

In one photo, the happy girl sits at a table surrounded by smiling faces. She smiles too and hangs her arm around another's shoulder. Also on the desk are a closed laptop, an open notebook with scribbled cartoons, and a stack of books: herbology, crystal magic, and modern witchcraft. Against the desk, a backpack sits open on the floor. Folders, notebooks, and pens spill out.

I grab a lanyard off the desk; Darkhaven Public Library is written on the strap. I stare at the girl in the picture on the ID badge. Her long brown hair rests in soft waves next to her face. Her smile stretches from ear to ear.

"I look so happy," I whisper.

"You were," a voice says from behind me.

I drop the lanyard and spin around, stumbling backward until I'm flush against the wall.

"Are you still happy, Ava? Are they . . . taking care of you?"

The woman standing before me is the same woman from the broken picture frame. She's the older woman who was holding the happy girl.

I shake my head, unable to believe we still have this psychic connection even after my death. Tears threaten, and I gasp, "Mamá."

She smiles at me and waits for me to answer her question.

"*Estoy asustado*," I whisper.

"You mustn't be afraid," Mamá replies.

"*Pero estoy sola*," I say.

"No. You're never alone. *Siempre estaré contigo*," she says as she walks toward me and plants a kiss atop my head.

I nod, and she wipes away my tears. She'll always be with me, but sometimes it's nice to hear it aloud. I feared she hated me after what happened.

"*No más llanto, mija*. Be strong. *Siempre te querré*."

"I love you too, Mamá."

❖

I wake in darkness, in solitude. Mamá is gone. Our psychic connection was broken when she abruptly severed our link. I didn't think she could still enter my dreams. That is a coveted ability between spirit users, but I'm not supposed to be a spirit witch anymore.

I think about what she said. She told me to be strong, and she asked if they were taking care of me. She might have cast me away, but I'm still her only child. She still cares, so she might allow me to return once I've learned control. The thought makes me giddy and ready to start my day.

I roll over in bed. The subtle sounds of an old, creaking

house echo in my mind. If I were blind, I might believe I'm home. The muffles of an old manor sound the same no matter where I am. But I'm not blind, and I'm not home. Having just visited my old bedroom, that thought sits heavily with me.

I sit up, shifting beneath the bundles of blankets that cocoon me. I brush a hand through my matted hair and scan the room. It's exactly the same as it was yesterday, when Jasik plopped me on the bed and told me I needed to rest. He offered to stay with me, but I needed space. I could tell he was unsure if he should trust me to stay put, but in the end, my insistence was stronger than his willpower.

With thick shades hanging over the windows, darkness engulfs my room, yet I can see everything, as if the sun is setting, casting shadows in corners while illuminating patches of floorboards.

The bedroom is stunning. The enormity of the furniture makes the room feel small, yet comforting and homey.

The king-size bed is dressed in a dark-beige comforter. It's supported by four posts that nearly touch the ceiling. Sheer white fabric twirls around each bedpost and then encloses the bed, creating a blissful paradise.

An enormous armoire nearly takes up one entire wall. I consider putting my clothes away, but I can't bring myself to admit I'll be staying long enough for the need to unpack.

An elegant makeup table is against another wall. Unfortunately, I don't wear much makeup, so that piece of furniture is pretty much a waste.

I lean against the headboard and stare at my overnight bag. The duffel is sitting on the floor beside the door. Inside are all the things I can never have. I contemplate opening it and attempting to wear my cross, but I'm not sure what scares me more—*thinking* I can't wear it or *confirming* the assumption.

I exhale sharply and try to clear my mind. My stomach is rumbling, and last night, Jasik informed me I'd need to feed today if I expect to survive the transition. I wasted too much of the wolf's blood to consider it an actual feeding.

I still want to survive the events of the full moon ritual, and unfortunately, becoming the undead is the only way to do that.

Much like my former bedroom, there are three doors to this room—one leads to the hallway, another leads to a closet, and the final leads to a small bathroom. I did some minor exploring after Jasik left last night, but I was too scared to venture outside my room. That's something I'll get to enjoy today, but this time I'll have a tour guide and won't really be sneaking around.

The walls are painted a dark blue, and the hardwood floors are stained dark chocolate brown. I didn't see much of the manor when Jasik carried me inside; I was too concerned with the fact that I had been stabbed by my new leader. But based on a few side glances, I can see this bedroom mirrors much of the house's other rooms. Clearly the vampires here favor antiques, natural wood, and dark colors.

Jasik mentioned that nearly a dozen vampires call Darkhaven home—and they all live here. He insists I've never met them on my patrols, which is a thought that never occurred to me. I'm glad I never tried to kill one of the vampires who live here. That might make things awkward.

I dangle my legs over the side of the bed and stretch involuntarily. My joints are stiff, my head aches, and my stomach is on a constant grumble loop. My mind is foggy. All I can really focus on is getting something to eat to calm my nerves. Jasik warned me that starvation affects vampires differently. Unlike humans, they don't just slowly die; they go mad from hunger. I was irrational immediately after my transition, and I don't want to risk lives by waiting too long to feed.

I hop off the bed, grab my duffel, and head for the bathroom. I plop my bag down, carefully unzip it, pull out an outfit that looks eerily similar to the one I'm already wearing, and toss my toiletry kit onto the counter. I leave everything else in the bag.

Staring at a set of crimson irises, I lean against the countertop. Stopping just inches away from the mirror, I curl my lips and run my tongue over my teeth, lingering on the pointy tips of my fangs. They are retracted, but they hang ever so slightly lower than a human's canines, giving away their hopeless attempt at normality.

Everything inside me screams that fangs are meant for ripping through flesh. Fangs mean death. Fangs mean *murder*. Vampires need blood to survive. *I* need blood to survive. Whether that means killing a human or an animal, it leaves an acidic sting in my gut.

No matter how I try to justify my actions and situation, my desire to kill is wrong. I should know better. It's immoral. But can vampires have morals? Witches fight for morals, for life. Vampires fight for blood . . . *for life*. The sickening twist on words leaves a bad taste in my mouth.

I pull away from the mirror and shake my head. I swallow hard and grab a tube of toothpaste.

After brushing, I jump in the shower, letting the water rush down my body and swirl into the drain at my feet. I curl my toes and then shoot them forward, flinging water as they return to their natural position.

When I'm done showering, I step out of the glass enclosure and wrap myself in a towel. I pad across the bathroom floor, leaving a trail of wet footprints in my wake, and quickly dress. My dirty clothes are in a pile on the bathroom floor, and I decide I'll come back for them later.

I twist my hair into a French braid that wraps around my shoulder and rests against my chest.

I carry my duffel into the bedroom and drop it onto the bed. Carefully, I remove the small, thin black box, and I open it to reveal my stake. I've hunted countless vampires with this very weapon by my side. It has never disappointed me.

I remove the weapon and let the weight sit in the palm of my hand. It's heavier than I remember. The sleek matte gray silver is cool against my skin. Running my thumb over the engraved runes, bumpy under my touch, sends shock waves down my spine.

This weapon was crafted to kill vampires, and I've just become one of them.

It's doused in witch magic, but that only aids the witch in defeating the vampire, a naturally stronger assailant. It's not necessary to actually kill one, especially if the user has enhanced vampire skills. I may not be able to tap into the magic encased within the stake, but I can certainly use it to pierce a heart, which is one of the few ways to kill a vampire.

I place the weapon back into its box and set it in my bag. Leaving it behind, I make my way toward the door, hesitating just before grabbing the knob. What if there are vampires in the hallway? Did Amicia make some kind of announcement, or will I surprise them? I press my ear to the door and listen for evidence that I'm not alone, but all I hear is silence. Maybe I'm the only one awake. After all, I'm not used to sleeping during the day and staying awake at night. It could still be early for vampires.

I turn the knob, poke my head into the hallway, and look around. Satisfied I won't run into anyone, I slip out of my bedroom and close the door behind me.

I tiptoe down the hallway in search of Jasik's room. Last night, before he left, he mentioned he was across the hall. But which room is his?

I reach a door, and just when I build up the courage to knock, someone interrupts me.

"Come in," someone says. I recognize it to be Jasik's voice. I'm instantly soothed by him. With my nerves at ease, I confidently enter.

Quickly, I turn the handle and step inside, closing the door behind me. I'm so pleased with myself, I don't consider the fact that I've just rushed into a vampire's room in the middle of the night.

I glance around. Jasik's bedroom is almost identical to my own. However, a few things stick out as being solely his. The walls are painted a deep maroon; it's just a couple shades darker than blood. Stacks of books are piled on the floor next to an overflowing bookshelf. Their musty smell fills the room with a familiar, homey aroma. The walls are decorated with pictures of cities and landscapes—each beautiful in its own way. A city skyline, a country cabin, mountains, and oceans, their diverse images have one common theme: a sunrise.

An easel with a half-finished painting is nestled in the corner. A color palette with splashes of paint sits on a table beside it. An overhead light illuminates the art. This piece doesn't look anything like the scenic paintings hanging on the walls. Instead, it features splashes of black and gray with two crimson circles. It's a close-up portrait of someone—clearly a vampire—but who? The curves of her face are soft, and the angle of her jaw is made of sharp, edgy lines. Her lips are ruby red, and she's smiling. Something about her feels too familiar. I stare at the painting until I can't bear to any longer.

I search the room for Jasik. Shirtless, he stands next to his bed. His hair is damp, and water droplets trickle down his forehead. Thick layers of muscle cover his torso. Evidence of his earlier assault from Amicia is gone. His skin healed over, not even leaving a scar as proof of her anger.

My heart thumps faster as I admire his body.

His chest rises and falls quickly, matching my own breath. His arms dangle at his sides, his hands clenched with white knuckles. My vision blurs; the space between us, though distant, feels somehow intimate.

"I'll just—I'll wait outside," I say, quickly turning away and grabbing on to the door handle.

He says nothing as I slip out the door and slam it behind me. Leaning against the wall, I tip my head back and close my eyes, waiting for my sputtering heart to slow.

What is wrong with me? I hate what I've become. I hate that a vampire has some warped control over me. But I can't deny the attraction.

After several deep breaths, I open my eyes to find Jasik beside me, his eyes hard, concerned.

"Time for a tour? A meet 'n' greet? Breakfast?" I say, spitting out whatever words form. I'm silently praying he won't mention that I saw him nearly naked or that it took far too many passing seconds for me to gather my thoughts and walk away.

My arm brushes against his as I walk around him. The tiny hairs rise, and a tingle shoots through my body. I gnaw on my lower lip to ignore the sensations.

I glance back and notice his gaze trailing my body. As his gaze lingers, I feel oddly vulnerable. Purely instinctual, I stand straighter, noticing how my leggings are a little too tight—and so is my top.

Our gazes meet, and he smiles, offering a grin that makes my heart stop. I focus on the two subtle dimples on either cheek, the strong line of his jaw, and the five o'clock shadow that ages him perfectly.

My breath catches as his eyes burn into mine, their crimson glow growing brighter with each second that passes. He wets his lips. Time drags on forever before he finally takes the few steps toward me.

I back away until I'm against the wall, not sure I am ready for him, for *this*. He stops when he reaches me, leaving only one step between us. His breathing is slow, heavy, matching my own. His eyes invite me to him, and as much as they beg me to accept his invitation, I don't know if I can.

I could lose myself in him; I know this. The twisted bond that unites us isn't the only thing working against me. I'm starting to respect Jasik. He's only tried to help me, and the few times my hunger took over, he stopped me from making mistakes I'd regret the rest of my life. And eternity is a long time to hate myself.

I'm realizing what I fear more than vampires—more than my coven finding out about this forbidden attraction, more than fighting a thousand rogue vampires at once—is that my once-insatiable appetite for hunting vampires is so easily subdued by my growing attraction for the man standing before me.

My body feels ready. My heart feels ready. But my mind tells me this is wrong. I was raised to shun vampires. I was forced to hate them. I need to remember that vampires are the reason I'm miles away from my home. Vampires did this to me, to my coven. I need to remember *who I am*.

Jasik reaches for me, his thumb rubbing against the angle of my jawline, sending shivers through my body.

"Ava," he whispers. In that one word, he says so many things. His voice, his plea, betrays his longing for me. Clearly I'm not the only one affected by our situation. Since there aren't hordes of women following him around, I have to assume I'm the first human he's turned.

I can feel Jasik's eyes on me, but I can't look at him. I walk away, leaving him behind. I don't know what to say or what to do. In my heart, Jasik feels good, real. In a world where I question everything I am, everything I know to be true, I don't question him. The way he looks at me, the way he says my name, the way he protected me in front of his own sire... I know there is something there. A simple attraction that could grow into an epic love that lasts until the end of time. Am I foolish to believe in such fairy tales?

I shake my head. I have to keep my mission in mind. I'm only here to learn control so I can return home. And that's what I want, right? I want to be reunited with my coven. I need to remind myself that my emotions are heightened because I'm a vampire. And I only feel this instant attraction for Jasik because he sired me. When I break down everything that's happened to the bare bones of it, that makes sense. But when we're alone, I want to say screw the witches and let's run off into the sunset together.

Oh, that's right. We can't. We're *vampires*.

I guess I really was played by the idea of a fairy-tale ending.

I really suck at being a vampire.

"You should feed," Jasik says when he reaches my side.

I nod and follow him down the hallway, eternally thankful he's not mentioning our almost indiscretion. We reach the stairs and take them down to the first-floor landing, which leads to a sitting room. Bookshelves line the walls, and an overstuffed couch and two matching chairs complete the room. The room is lit by a couple of lamps on side tables. The dim lighting is just enough for me to see everything clearly.

"This way," Jasik says, ushering me through the manor.

We turn left and walk through a large dining room with an attached wood-burning fireplace. It's not lit, and I wonder if they ever actually use it. Vampires don't get cold, and fire isn't really a friend. Even so, the stonework around the fireplace is beautiful.

A large stained-glass window overlooks an overgrown garden. The night sky is dark, and the moon is waning above the world.

The long farmhouse-style table could easily sit the dozen or so vampires who call the manor home. It's breakfast time, so I'm sure I'll have to meet a few more at some point today. I'm dreading that encounter more than I'm dreading feeding time.

In the back left corner of the dining room, a small butler's pantry leads to the kitchen. A massive refrigeration unit takes up most of the room. But my eyes are drawn elsewhere. To my right is a small sitting nook, where Jeremiah and Hikari are loudly slurping their morning snack.

Jasik nods at the two, who smile back at him. Jeremiah eyes me curiously, and I offer a pathetic half wave. I nearly die inside at our awkward interaction. I bet they're not sure where we stand or what my place within their nest will be. Amicia wasn't happy with Jasik, and I'm sure her mood swings affect her sires. I don't miss the fact that Hikari doesn't even look my way.

Jasik leads me to the refrigerator and opens the door. I take a peek at the seemingly endless rows of neatly stacked cases containing blood bags. Each bag is labeled with dates and blood type. Jasik grabs four bags before closing the door. He walks over to the counter, grabs two coffee mugs from the cabinet, and pours the contents into each mug. He pops those into the microwave to nuke at the same time my stomach begins turning to mush. His confident, easy strides at making a bloody breakfast are making me queasy.

When the timer dings, he grabs the mugs and offers one to me.

"Let's eat in the solarium," he suggests as he grabs the blood bags and tosses them into the trash.

I nod, thankful to get some space from the other vampires.

We exit the kitchen and enter the dining room. A few vampires have made their way downstairs, and I keep my gaze on the steaming cup of breakfast in my hands. They whisper to each other when they see me and then say hello to Jasik.

"The solarium wraps around the side of the house. You can enter it through the dining room, sitting room, and parlor," Jasik says.

"Isn't a solarium a little dangerous in a house full of vampires?" I ask. "I mean, a solarium is basically a huge sun-room. Whose idea was it to build a sun-room in a house made for vampires?"

"During the day, it can be deadly." Jasik chuckles. "But we

tend to sleep all day and take advantage of the room at night. Here. Hold this."

He hands me his mug o' blood and opens the sliding glass doors that connect the dining room to the solarium. He pushes the doors open until they're neatly tucked within the wall. He turns back to me, takes his mug, and waits for me to enter the room.

The solarium is wall-to-wall, floor-to-ceiling windows—most of which are the beautiful stained glass that the builder of this house clearly favored. The room is massive and wraps around the entire length of the manor. Several different seating areas are positioned throughout the room, and thankfully, only one vampire is currently occupying the space.

"Malik," Jasik says in greeting as we approach his brother.

Malik looks up, his face noticeably changing when his gaze lands on me. Like all the rest, he wears the what-is-she-really-doing-here face, and he wears it well. I wonder if I have that same look on my face when I see them. After all, it's a great question, because . . . what am I actually doing here? I'm a witch . . . in a vampire nest. I keep telling myself I'm here to learn control, but given the chance to leave, could I actually go?

"I see you made it through the night," Malik says. He takes a large gulp from his mug and waits for me to respond.

"Was not surviving really an option?" I say, concerned.

"He means to say he's happy you're *still* here," Jasik clarifies.

"I *mean* I'm surprised you didn't run away in the middle of the night," Malik counters. I don't miss the fact that he dropped the word "happy."

"Why would I run away? I chose to come with you," I say.

I still haven't taken a sip of my breakfast, and I'm beginning to wonder if the other vampires have noticed yet.

"Be honest with yourself, Ava. You didn't *choose* anything. Your family forced you out," Malik argues.

I bite my tongue. His accusation upsets me, but that doesn't make it any less true. My coven did what they've always done: run in the face of something they don't understand. Instead of trying to learn from it, they assume it's bad. One day, they'll realize that even though I'm a vampire, I'm still *me*. Aside from the raging hormones and enhanced senses, I don't feel any different. I'm still the girl who would die to protect them.

"Malik," Jasik warns. His voice is sharp, his speech to the point.

I offer him a thankful glance.

"Have a seat," he says.

I pull out the metal chair, which scrapes against the tile floor, and set down my mug on the table. I still haven't taken a sip. Jasik eyes it curiously before downing the rest of his breakfast. Malik follows suit.

"You need to feed," Jasik says. His voice is soft, concerned.

"I know."

"It won't be like last time," he says.

"The more you feed, the easier it becomes. And you need to learn control," Malik adds.

I eye the cup. The liquid content is deep red in color and still warm to my touch. A perfect ninety-eight degrees? I cringe at the thought. I can't think about where it came from. I just need to gulp it down and call it a day. As much as I don't like the idea, I believe them when they tell me it'll get easier.

With a dramatic sigh, I lift the mug to my lips and drink

deep. Like with the wolf, the taste isn't what I was expecting. It's thick and creamy and goes down smooth. The blood tastes sweet with just a hint of spice. It doesn't quite taste as raw and real as the wolf's blood, but it's delicious nonetheless.

When I finish, I set the mug on the counter and lick my blood mustache from my upper lip.

"You'll start to feel better," Jasik says. "Your mind is clearer when you're not hungry."

I suppose that's a plus. The last thing I need is for my hunger to take control. I may be a vampire, but I don't want to hurt anyone.

"So what happens now?" I ask. I slide my empty mug away from me and lean back in my chair.

"We should begin training," Malik says.

I arch a brow. "Training? For what?"

"You must train physically to learn what it means to be a vampire. This was my promise to Amicia," he clarifies.

I shake my head. "I don't need to learn how to fight. I *know* how to fight. I went on nightly patrols and hunted…" I clear my throat. "I know how to fight, Malik."

"You don't know how to fight *like a vampire*. You're stronger than before, and your senses are heightened. This will be a challenge for you in battle."

"Look, I can take care of myself. I just need you to help me control my blood lust. That's it."

Malik leans close, folding his arms over the tabletop, and says, "Unfortunately, little one, you'll only learn that with time."

TEN

At some point, I'll have to agree to train with Malik, but something inside me is finding joy in avoiding him. It's like some sick, twisted game, and the prize is a frustrated vampire.

I suppress a chuckle as Malik leaves the room, annoyed that I'm still refusing to train with him. Eventually he'll realize that I don't need him to teach me self-defense. That ship sailed long ago.

I believed him when he told me I'd only learn to control my blood lust with time, but hearing it aloud still sucks. I don't want to spend years perfecting my ability not to kill someone. My coven doesn't have *years* to wait for me. They're mortal. With each passing day, they're closer to an inevitable demise. And being witches, the mortal enemies of vampires, doesn't help their cause. They're targets, making them all the more likely to die young.

Briefly, I allow myself to believe there can be peace among the Darkhaven supernaturals. As much as I'd love to formally introduce my former coven and my new nest-mates, I'm thinking getting everyone to agree to a sit-down meeting will also take time. It seems everything I want to do has a long shelf life.

"How are you feeling?" Jasik asks, interrupting my thoughts.

I shrug in response.

"It's hard in the beginning. The transition takes a heavy toll. The more you feed, the easier everything becomes."

"Like what?" I ask.

"Your mind will clear. You won't feel as conflicted about your choices."

"Meaning what? My natural instincts will take over?"

He nods. "That's a good way to put it."

"But aren't my natural instincts to kill? I am a vampire now."

This time, he shrugs. "I don't know. Were you a killer before I bit you?" He tries to hide his coy smile, but I'm not finding him funny. He doesn't know how true his words are to me.

"Not exactly."

He leans toward me and rests his elbows on the tabletop. The moonlight is shining through the stained-glass windows, illuminating the space around him. His pale skin shines in the dark, and his crimson irises glow even brighter.

"Ava—"

He shakes his head and runs a hand through his soft brown hair. I can tell he's struggling to find the right words, so I brace myself for what he's about to say.

"You have to stop thinking of vampirism as being some virus intent on wiping out earth's population."

I cross my arms against my chest and lean back. The metal chair is cool beneath my T-shirt.

"If vampirism isn't an infection, what is it? How should I think of what's happened to me?" I ask.

"Vampirism has elevated your natural existence. It's making you a better, stronger, smarter ... you. If you were a killer before you turned, then yes, you're going to be an evil rogue vampire now."

"And you kill rogues?"

He nods. "But if you were just a regular person trying to survive in a difficult world, you'll be fine."

"But I wasn't a regular person. I was a witch intent on ending the vampire species. I was born into this blood war."

"And now you live for it," Jasik responds. "Blood is your life now."

"Don't you think my experiences mean I don't have the luxury of time? I need to learn to control my blood lust *now*. I almost killed my coven, those kids." I shake my head in frustration. Why am I the only one who thinks waiting is a bad idea?

"You were newly born. You weren't yourself."

"That's no excuse."

"I'm not giving you an excuse. That's the reason you acted the way you did. Your emotions are heightened. Already, I'm sure you feel a bit on edge. You'll be riding an emotional roller coaster for a while, Ava. You can't blame yourself for your misdeeds while your head is foggy. Transitioning into a new level of existence isn't easy."

"When will I feel normal again?" I ask.

He exhales sharply. "It's important that you know I'll never lie to you—even when the truth hurts."

What is that supposed to mean? I eye him cautiously and wait for him to continue.

"I'm not sure you'll ever feel like you did when you were just a witch. That's like asking the fish to feel like the worm, the poor to feel rich, minorities to feel like the majority. You're asking one being to feel an unrealistic amount of empathy.

There's only so much we can understand when we try to put ourselves in someone else's situation."

"So I'll never feel . . . normal again?"

"I'm not saying that. I'm saying your definition of 'normal' is going to change. Your idea of feeling like yourself is going to be redefined. You won't feel like a mortal witch because you're not one anymore. But if you give it a chance, you just might find that feeling like a vampire isn't so bad."

We remain silent for several minutes, and I appreciate Jasik allowing me to digest what he said before throwing a wicked curve ball my way. There's only so much new information I can handle in one day.

"I am, you know," I say.

"Hmm?" he asks.

"I am willing to try. I'm not going to lie to you either. I never wanted to be a vampire, and most of the time, I still don't want to be one. Not a minute passes when I don't wish I could just go home, take it all back. I wish I'd stayed inside instead of patrolling. I never would have met that vampire. He never would have come back. We wouldn't have been attacked, and you never would have interrupted our ritual to save me. I'd be sleeping in my own bed right now. I'd spend tomorrow with Liv. I'd . . ." I swallow hard and stare off into space. It's safe to say I kind of hate my life right now.

"I'm sorry you can't spend tomorrow with friends and family. I'm sorry you won't grow old with them and die a mortal death."

"Eternity is a long time to be alone," I whisper.

He nods. "It is. I often forget how blessed I am. I'm never alone. Malik is my biological brother. So few are this lucky."

"Will you tell me about your life?" I ask.

He's silent for a moment before responding. "We lived in a small seaside village in England. My father was a cottager, and my mother cared for my brother and me. We had a small cottage to call home but no land, so my father took odd jobs working on other people's land so we could survive. We didn't have enough money to buy our own goat for milk and cheese or chickens for eggs. So my mother would often barter for food. She was an amazing seamstress."

I smile and wait for him to continue.

"There were so many feral cats in my village. They helped keep the rodents at bay. We never worried about infestations the way some of the finer properties did. I became friendly with one particular cat. She was pregnant, so I would save scraps of food when I could. Eventually she trusted me enough to take them straight from my hand."

"That's sweet," I say.

"The merchant ships brought the vermin that carried the plague. It didn't take long to reach our little village. Since I spent most of my days caring for feral cats . . ."

He exhales slowly, and my breath nearly catches as I wait for him to continue.

"It didn't take much time to spread from me to my family. Malik and I lost everything and everyone in one fatal swoop. Amicia came to us in the middle of the night. When we awoke the next day, she was still there, and we felt so much better. We believed she saved us, but our parents weren't as fortunate. They died that same night. With nothing left for us, we left with Amicia and eventually settled here."

"Jasik . . . I don't know what to say. I'm so sorry," I whisper. He might have died several hundred years ago, but it's clear the pain of that experience still very much lives within him. I can relate to that. The pain of losing my coven and my life will probably never leave me.

"As tragic as my life has been, I won't pretend to understand your confusion, your pain. The day I awoke as a vampire, I left home. My family remains as memories in my mind, and I'm grateful I don't still live somewhere where I am constantly reminded of everything I lost that fateful evening."

I stare at Jasik as he recounts his transition. He falls silent, and his eyes grow dark. I'm certain he's reliving moments he probably wishes remained buried. Guilt stabs me for just asking him to share his past with me.

"Amicia saved our lives, and for several centuries, we've remained loyal to her."

"You don't have a choice, do you? She's your sire."

Our gazes meet. "Siring someone doesn't eliminate free will. You're not bound to my word, Ava. You're free, and I'll never stop you if you wish to leave."

"But I *feel* something," I whisper.

"We are blood bound, but it's a superficial link." He waves off my concern with his hand. "You aren't fated to me just because I turned you."

"Then why was Amicia so concerned when I arrived?"

"It's nothing more than a power play."

"But you just said the sire bond doesn't really matter," I counter.

"No, I said the sire bond doesn't grant me control over you. You still have free will. But we are linked. I've never met a sired pair of vampires who didn't care for each other. If we are each other's priority, there isn't much room for Amicia."

I consider his words. Deep down, I do feel that spark. There's a growing attraction, a lingering pebble of respect for

Jasik. If this is all the sire bond entails, I think I can control it. I can wield it to benefit me while I remain with the vampires.

But I can't deny that there's something more. A sense of loyalty is beginning to form as I get to know the vampire before me and the human he used to be. I want so desperately to return to my coven, but I'm hurt that they would forsake me so easily. Ever since our first encounter, Jasik has been by my side, caring for me, nurturing my vampirism, and even protecting me from his own sire. I do believe he won't force me to stay, and I'm not even sure if leaving is the right thing to do. It feels like I'm becoming more confused with each hour that passes.

And maybe, *just maybe*, being a witch-turned-vampire won't be so bad.

"Are you hungry?" Jasik asks, breaking my concentration.

At some point, I picked up my empty blood mug and started spinning it in my hands. I was so focused on everything he said, I didn't even realize I was doing this.

I shake my head and push the mug away. "No."

He arches a brow. "Are you sure? I know it's hard at first, but you really need to feed when you're hungry. The first several days are crucial."

"I was just thinking."

"About?" he asks.

I don't want to admit my feelings for him are turning from immediate hate to sort-of-kind-of-*maybe* like. I also don't want him to know that I'm still torn about my coven, so I spit out the first lie that comes to mind.

I nod at the doorway behind him. "What's in that room?"

The door is closed, and I know it leads to a room I haven't seen. The conservatory is one massive L-shaped room that connects to all the first-floor rooms on the right side of the manor. That mystery room should be located to the right of the foyer, so I'm guessing it's nothing exciting. But it's a viable distraction.

Jasik glances over his shoulder, and I admire the way his muscles strain beneath his T-shirt. I shake my head as I look away, chastising myself. Jasik has already confirmed that the sire bond is superficial, so I can stop this nonsense *right now*.

"That's the parlor," he responds before facing me again.

"And that would be?"

"A fancy name for a living room."

I nod. "Can I see it?"

He shrugs. "Sure."

He loops his fingers between the handles of our mugs and carries them as he stands. He pushes in his chair and then my chair before walking me toward the closed door. Clearly chivalry is not dead. It's alive and well in this nearly seven-hundred-year-old vampire.

"Technically, you can get to the parlor from the foyer and the sitting room. That's why this door pretty much stays closed."

He opens the door and ushers me inside. Another stone fireplace sits as the room's main focal point. Two large couches box it in, and on the far wall, a chess table is positioned in front of large bay windows that overlook the front yard. I can see the stone path that leads to the porch and the woods in the distance.

"Who plays?" I ask, eyeing the unfinished chess game.

He snorts. "Malik and I have been playing that game for three years. He won't make a move because he refuses to lose to me."

I grin and think about Liv. That's definitely something she would do. Heck, even I would do that, but that would mean she was winning. And she and I both know board games are my forte.

I walk over to the game and kneel down. I blow at the dust that has coated the pieces and laugh.

"This definitely doesn't feel like a vampire nest," I say as I stand and turn to face him. Jasik still stands across the room by the doorway we entered through.

"What were you expecting?"

"A dungeon," I say as I walk toward him.

He offers a hearty laugh, and I smile. In the last day and a half, I've only seen concern from him. It's nice to see him relax around me. I'm sure it's not easy. It's hard for me to lower my walls around vampires, but Jasik makes it pretty easy. I'm sure it's the sire bond, but I'm a little grateful. If I were on guard twenty-four-seven, I'd lose my mind.

I scan the rest of the room, and my gaze lands on the large painting positioned above the fireplace. Immediately I can see it is supposed to be Amicia. It's not a clear portrait, but instead, it's like the unfinished painting in Jasik's bedroom. Splashes of paint form her delicate features, from the soft curve of her nose to her prominent lips to her alluring eyes.

"That's beautiful," I say.

Jasik doesn't speak as I walk over to the painting and reach up, trailing my fingers softly against the canvas. Thick lines of paint dried as rigid edges. I shiver as one scrapes against my fingertips.

"I've always admired art, but I've never had the talent," I say as I turn to face Jasik. "Have you always been an artist?"

His jaw clenches. The tiny muscles bulge, and I find

my gaze narrowing in on his neck. A thick vein protrudes, tantalizing, teasing. I clear my throat and quickly look away. I don't wait for him to answer as I find something else to home in on.

Several bookshelves are lined against the remaining wall. Unlike the shelves in Jasik's bedroom, these are neatly stacked with leather-bound classics. As I approach the shelves, the smell of books becomes overwhelming and clouds my senses. They smell of age, of strength and dedication.

They smell like home, and the memories come flooding in. We also have a small library in our house. The witch elders would teach the young the ways of our people and the threat of the vampire race. I remember sitting on the floor with my legs crisscrossed, eagerly listening to tales that were passed down from generation to generation. We used to spend a couple hours each night in the library, listening to stories, researching vampires, and learning our history.

The older I became, the more Mamá pushed me to learn everything I could so that I could one day become an elder in our coven. She even hoped I'd become the high priestess one day. But eventually I grew tired of stories and games. I ventured out to experience life for myself and started patrolling and training harder than ever. I was devoted to protecting my coven, not leading it.

The books sit neatly on the shelves, squeezed into spots that seem too small for the bindings. One catches my eye. Unlike the others, it's not perfectly bound in a leather cover. It's old, stained, and bound together by stitching, not glue. This book hasn't been cared for like the others. Why?

I wiggle the book free. Its fabric cover is peeling, as is the threaded binding. As I flip through the yellowed pages, I notice that most are no longer attached to the spine. I close the book and run my fingertips against the divots of the title. I carefully place the book back on the shelf, gently securing it in its fragile state next to the others. Maybe whoever stored it here thinks it is safe between the other books. When it was alone in my hands, it looked too fragile, like it would easily be destroyed, but now, among the many books, it's protected.

I look down at my hands and then back to the book. Its torn cover gives away its hiding spot. Can it truly be safe beside the others? Or is this one book in greater danger because of its uniqueness?

I can't help but compare our situations. I may be a vampire, but does that mean I'm truly safe here?

✦

Jasik and I are finally settling into a not-so-awkward silence when Hikari comes barging into the parlor. Her eyes are narrowed, with laser beams aimed directly at my heart. She's so furious I almost want to take cover.

She storms into the room, causing Jasik to stand so abruptly the novel he was reading falls from his hand and smacks against the hardwood floor. I wince as it lands in a loud *thump*.

Hikari throws something at me, and I reach for it instinctively. I grab on to the canvas bag just as it falls into my lap.

It's my overnight bag. I'm staring at the inner contents of the bag I packed when I was booted from my house and offered refuge here, where the vampires are oh-so-welcoming.

My gaze darts between Hikari and my bag. I'm confused

by her anger and the unspoken accusation hanging in the air.

Has she been going through my stuff? Why would she go into my room without permission? What was she looking for?

"Hikari, what's going on?" Jasik asks.

"Why don't you ask *her*," she responds, her gaze never leaving mine.

"Ava?" Jasik asks. He seems just as confused as I am. I'm glad to know he didn't have any part of this intrusion on my privacy.

"This is my bag. Were you going through my stuff?" I zip the bag and throw the strap over my shoulder as I stand.

Hikari is around my height, and she's just as naturally thin. I'm so upset by her brazen behavior, I'm certain I can take her in a fight. I'm fuming from anger, and what little trust Jasik and I were establishing has just been blown to pieces. If Hikari could do this, how do I know the other vampires aren't working behind my back? For all I know, Amicia put her up to this. Maybe they're *all* out to get me.

"Yes," Hikari says simply.

"Hikari," Jasik says, his tone sharp. He's upset with her and on my side, which makes me smile.

"I had good reason, Jasik. Why don't you ask her what's hiding in her bag?"

He's about to object, but something stops him. I suppose he's considering her words, and either curiosity or fear is getting the best of him. He faces me.

"Ava?"

"What?" I snap.

"What's in your bag?" he asks calmly.

"Nothing! You were there. I had two minutes to pack and leave. I took what I could before we were all incinerated by fire magic. You both should be thanking me for not taking my time!"

I'm furious that Hikari would dare not only to go through *my* stuff but also to try to turn Jasik against me. He's my only ally in a house full of vampires who aren't fond of guests—or witches. The minute I lose him, I'm ousted. And where am I going to go? I'm penniless, and I certainly can't live on the streets with hunger creeping in every hour.

"Lies! I *saw* them. Admit it!" Hikari shouts, garnering the attention of nearby vampires. I've never seen these few before, and I'm fairly certain this is an awful way to make first introductions. Now they're going to be suspicious of me too—even if Hikari's accusations are unfounded. I mean, honestly, who will they believe? A vampire who's fought to protect them from rogues, or me, a witch-turned-vampire who barged in last night and hasn't left.

"All I packed were clothes, bathroom stuff, a photo album, and . . ." I trail off as I consider the final two items in my bag.

Huh. It never occurred to me that those two particular items could be blown out of proportion. This could be a bad situation for me.

"*And what?*" Hikari urges. Her black pixie locks are wildly styled, matching her fiery temper. The gelled points of her short hair mirror the very thing she fears.

I sigh. "And a cross and stake."

The vampires nearby gasp as they back away. They rush from the room, probably on their way to get Amicia. If I don't clear this up quickly, I'm definitely a goner—and maybe in the permanent way.

"It's not what you think," I say as I step forward. Hikari steps back, but Jasik remains still. He's staring at me with disbelief. The betrayal strewn across his face guts me.

"Admit it, Ava," Hikari says. "You still have connections to those witches. How can we trust you? You knew you were coming to a vampire nest, and you chose to bring two items that can *kill us!*"

"Hikari, you need to calm down," I groan. "The cross is a necklace. That's not doing much damage."

"What do you think happens when we touch that thing? We combust!" she argues.

"Well then, don't try it on, and you shouldn't be touching my stuff anyway!" I snap back.

"Why would you bring those things here?" Jasik asks, ignoring our all-out cat fight.

"Because she's still siding with the witches! She probably planned all of this. Now she knows *where we live*, Jasik. Bringing her here was a deadly mistake. This time, you've gone too far."

Jasik ignores her and says, "How do you expect us to trust you after you brought those things here? Didn't you think we'd find out?"

"I *promise* I didn't mean any harm. I don't want to hurt anyone," I say as I side-eye Hikari. She just might be my exception, but I don't admit to that aloud.

"Then why bring them?" he asks.

"I couldn't leave them behind, especially not the cross necklace. It was a gift from Papá. It's all I have left of him."

"And the stake?" he continues.

I shake my head as I search for an explanation, but I can't find one. "I don't know. Habit, I guess. I bring that thing everywhere. It's like my arm. I can't go anywhere without that either."

Hikari snorts loudly, and I roll my eyes. She's probably imagining ripping off my arm right now. Silently, I dare her. I'd use it to beat her to a bloody pulp.

"You can't seriously believe her, Jasik," Hikari says.

"I didn't come here with any intention of hurting anyone. I only came to learn from you," I say.

"Then why not agree to training with Malik?" he counters.

I curse internally. I knew my defiance would come back to bite me in the butt.

"Because I don't want to waste my time something I already know how to do. I just want to learn to control my blood lust so I won't be a threat to them anymore," I shout. I'm erratic and speaking so quickly I don't even have time to consider my words before I say them.

"A threat to whom?" Jasik asks.

"To my coven!" I shout, flailing my arms around like a total psycho.

"Aha!" Hikari shouts. "So you admit it! You were planning to return to them. It's been your plan all along, hasn't it? Did you plan to just use us and dump us? Were you going to make us trust you and then share our secrets with the witches?"

I open my mouth to speak, but no words come out. I glance between the growing number of onlooking vampires before my gaze finally rests on Jasik. Earlier today, Jasik promised me he'd never lie to me, so lying to get out of this mess just seems wrong.

"I'm sorry," I whisper to him.

"So am I," he says before walking away and leaving me alone in a room with a half-dozen angry vampires.

ELEVEN

It doesn't take much for Jasik to clear the room. The vampires here listen to him like their lives may depend on his orders. I suppose they're used to him protecting them, but I hope he doesn't expect me to be quite so submissive.

He glances at me, his eyes unreadable, before walking into the foyer and out the front door. I assume I'm supposed to follow him, so I practically run from the room in case the other vampires decide to double back and have a not-so-nice chat with me. The last thing I need is to fight for my life when I'm already fighting for my life.

The night sky is dark, and the stars are bright. They're more than enough to light my path. The air is cool against my skin. It sweeps across the lawn and brushes against my cheeks, bringing the many scents of the earth with it. I remember a time when I could tap into the earth's power and wield it as my own. That kind of strength would help right about now.

Sometimes, I really miss being a witch.

Jasik is sitting on the stairs. The wraparound front porch is vacant except for the two of us, and I'm thankful Jasik's demeanor scared the other vampires away. I'd like the fewest number of eyes on us as possible.

Of course, there's nothing stopping the other vampires from eavesdropping, and if they really want to, they can probably hear us from the basement or third-floor attic. If I didn't think it'll one day help me in battle, I'd curse the vampire super-hearing.

The breeze brushes through Jasik's hair, blowing the brown locks toward me. I inhale deeply when his natural musk reaches my nose. Even his hair smells like cinnamon and summertime.

Slowly, I approach him from behind. I slide the strap from my luggage around my torso and push the bag behind me so it rests against my back. Missing only my outfit from last night, it's packed full and weighed down heavily.

If Jasik asks me to leave, I could. I have everything I need in my bag. I left that pile of clothes on the bathroom floor, but the only two things that matter are here with me. I'm not too worried about missing one outfit. I'm more worried about surviving without a mentor.

I need to do whatever I can to stay here, even if that means groveling. I just hope Amicia doesn't find out about my indiscretion. This could be the one mistake that costs me my life.

I watch Jasik carefully as I sit down beside him. He rests his long legs against the front porch stairs, his feet against the very bottom step. On the other hand, my short legs don't need quite as much room. I sit and rest my elbows on my knees.

Staring out into the distance, I can feel Jasik's gaze on me, but I don't move or speak. I wait until he's ready to talk about it—or simply *listen* to what I have to say.

"How long were you planning to stay with us?" he asks.

"Until I don't have to worry about the safety of my coven whenever I get hungry," I admit.

"So . . . forever?" he asks.

I look at him, our gazes locking, and see no sign of mischief or humor in his crimson eyes.

"What do you mean?" I ask when I realize he's not joking.

"You're never going to feel that confident around humans. Even I sometimes worry my hunger will get the best of me."

"Really?"

He nods. "I told you I'll never lie to you. Lying does us both a disservice, and even though I'm immortal, I haven't the time to waste on remembering pointless lies."

"You have no faith in me, do you?" I ask.

"This has nothing to do with faith, Ava. I have the experience you require. I know how much vampires yearn for the kill. You're a predator now. Mortals are your natural prey. There will never be a time when you won't fancy ripping out their hearts and sucking them dry."

I shudder at the thought. "Thanks for that detailed image." I'm not sure I'll be able to get that picture out of my head.

"I won't apologize. You need to understand how dangerous you are now."

I exhale slowly, loudly. The distant hum of wildlife echoes through the forest. I can hear the birds in the trees and the bugs in the ground. Who would have thought vampirism is truly a wonderful way to appreciate Mother Nature?

"I suppose that's why Malik is so insistent on training me," I say.

"It is," Jasik responds.

"Even though I'm not sure I need combat training," I argue. Eventually, if I say this enough, they might believe me and forget the idea of training with Malik. A girl can dream . . .

"You do."

"There you go again, having no faith. I'm pretty good at

what I do," I say. I don't need to remind him that I was my coven's hunter. I went on nightly patrols, and I only lost the one time. Granted, it was a pretty epic failure, but even weakened, I was a damn good warrior for the cause.

"One day, you'll understand that we speak of experience, not faith. We don't want you to make the mistakes we've made, and you don't have to—as long as you stop being so bloody stubborn and just trust us."

I chuckle. Only after Jasik told me about his past did I start to notice the subtle English accent that's been muffled by his many years in America. He's been in Darkhaven a lot longer than he was in England.

"Promise me something?" he says.

"What?" I ask.

The breeze picks up, blowing against the branches of a nearby tree. The leaves protest, and a rattling sound pierces my ears. If I close my eyes, the wind blowing through the forest sounds an awful lot like the waves of the sea. If there's one thing I'm beginning to appreciate, it's my enhanced hearing, even if eavesdroppers are annoying.

"Promise me you won't return to them unless you're absolutely positive you can control your hunger."

"But you have no faith in that ever happening."

Jasik smiles, and I tear my gaze away from him. I'm not sure why he's not as upset as the others. I thought Hikari was going to have an aneurysm. It's good to know Jasik will give me the benefit of the doubt, even when things look *really* bad.

"Well, you are incredibly stubborn. You just might be the one exception," he says.

I snort at his accusation. "You know, I just might. And yes, I promise. I have no intention of doing that anyway. It was hard for me to leave my coven and even harder for me to leave with *vampires*. It's not easy being a witch-turned-vampire."

"No, I imagine it's not. But you're doing a pretty good job," he says, comforting me.

"Really? I feel like I kind of suck at being a vampire."

"Well, if there's one thing vampires need to be good at, it's sucking."

I scoff and playfully smack his shoulder. "Did you just tell me a joke? I didn't think you were capable of real humor."

"No one understands my British humor, so I usually don't even try." He smiles, and my heart nearly melts.

"All kidding aside, I won't keep any more secrets from you," I say. "I never meant to lie to you. To be honest, I didn't feel like I was really hiding anything, and I figured you guys wanted me to leave as much as I wanted to go, so . . ." I shrug.

"It'll take time, but they'll get used to you. You're a vampire now. Your past doesn't matter."

"It seems to matter to Hikari. She doesn't trust me."

"Can you blame her? You brought a cross and stake into her home. She's protective of her family. I'm sure you'd feel the same if this were your home."

"Yeah, I guess. But she went at this all wrong."

"She did, but can you forgive her?"

I don't answer right away. I think about the situation. Yes, what she did was wrong, but Jasik is right. She was suspicious because she wants to protect her family. I can't blame her for that. I've done some pretty awful things in the name of loyalty to my coven.

"She shouldn't be judged by this one mistake," Jasik presses.

"I know. I guess I forgive her, but she needs to back off," I say.

He nods. "I'll talk to her."

"It's hard enough being the newbie here. I don't need her on my case."

"You speak like you care what the others think. I thought you didn't plan on being here long, so why does this even bother you?" Jasik asks.

"Well, according to you, I'll be here for at least a few hundred years."

"If we're lucky," he whispers. He smiles before looking away.

We're silent for a moment as I build the courage to tell him about my dream with Mamá. I'm about to break the lighthearted mood we have right now, but I agreed not to keep secrets. Besides, I'm a little shaken and a lot confused by the experience, and Jasik just might know what the heck is going on. I'm sure a witch-turned-vampire is a rare creature, but he's been around almost seven hundred years. If he hasn't encountered another vampire like me, then no one has.

"Jasik," I say. I wait for him to look at me before I continue. "There's something else you should know."

He frowns. "What is it?"

"Last night, something happened."

He sits upright, bringing his long legs to mirror my own. He rests his forearms on his thighs. "What happened? Did you leave your room?"

"No, but apparently that wouldn't matter anyway. The vampires here have personal boundary issues."

He groans and ignores my pointed remark. "What happened?"

"I was a spirit witch. My powers were rooted in my psyche, not the elements. One of the reasons spirit users are coveted is because we're considered psychic. One thing spirit witches can do that others cannot is enter the dreams of another spirit witch."

"Okay," he says slowly.

"Well, those powers should have been severed when I transitioned, right?" I ask.

He nods. "Yes, I suppose that makes sense. You're not a witch anymore. You're a vampire."

"It happened last night. I'm not sure if I entered hers or if she entered mine, but it was definitely a dream, and we were definitely both there."

"Who? Who is she?" he asks.

"Mamá," I say.

"Your mother? You're sure this was . . . that spirit thing and not an actual dream?" His voice is frantic, and his pulse escalates slightly. I understand he's concerned, but I'm not sure why. Is it because I accessed witch powers, or is it because the dream was with Mamá? What is he really afraid of?

"I'm positive. I can't explain it. A witch just *knows* when you're using spirit instead of having a real dream."

"Ava, you're not a witch."

"I—I know. I just mean . . . I used to do this all the time. I can tell the difference."

He nods but doesn't speak. His eyes seem vacant as he's lost in his thoughts. Maybe he's thinking back to his many years as a vampire and he's about to tell me exactly what's going on. I knew there was nothing to worry about.

"I don't understand what happened, but I don't want you to think I'm keeping secrets. I'm not even sure how it's possible," I say.

"This is something we need to look into. Perhaps Amicia has experience."

I'm certain my eyes are bulging from their sockets. "*Amicia?* You heard her last night. Any sign of trouble, and she'll kill us both for what you did. Maybe we shouldn't tell her about this. Or anyone. Let's just keep it between you and me. I mean, I'm sure it's nothing."

"Ava—" Jasik's tone is calm and soothing, but that doesn't last long.

"Jasik!" someone yells from behind us.

We both turn to find Malik running toward us. He runs through the sitting room and into the foyer. The front doors fling open, smacking against the house. I'm shocked the stained glass doesn't shatter on impact.

Jasik bolts upright, and I struggle to keep up. My bag is heavy against my chest. I claw at the strap to reposition it. The weight of it is more of a nuisance than anything else.

"What is it?" Jasik asks.

"Something's happened," Malik responds. His usual cool-and-collected demeanor is gone, and even I'm beginning to freak out. I'm not sure what's going on, but clearly, something is amiss. Malik is panicking, and the little time we've spent together has taught me that's a rare occurrence.

"What is it?" Jasik says, more forcefully this time.

"Humans have been attacked."

❖

The next several minutes pass by in a blur.

The vampires are getting ready so quickly I can't keep up with them. Hikari rushes past me, her shoulder jabbing into mine as she passes. Malik disappears in the blink of an eye, and I hear the distant rush of footsteps upstairs. I don't see Jeremiah. The last time I saw him was earlier at breakfast time. Hours have passed since then. Where is he? Is he involved?

Jasik grabs my hand and pulls me through the manor. No longer standing in the foyer, we rush through the open-layout sitting room and take the stairs two at a time until we reach the second-floor landing. Our bedrooms are just down the hallway. We run past a few lingering vampires who press against the wall as we pass. I'm not sure if they were trying to avoid *me* or if they were used to the hunters running through the house like madmen.

There seems to be order in this house. Everyone has a role. Amicia is their leader, and there are the vampires who simply live here, and then there are the hunters who protect them. Jasik is part of the latter, as are Malik, Hikari, and Jeremiah.

We reach Jasik's bedroom door in record time. He pulls me inside his room, and I bump into the jutting doorframe. A surge of pain rushes through me, but I ignore the sensation.

He slams closed the door behind us and drops my hand. My heart is pounding in my head, and my thoughts are spinning out of control. The energy of the house seeps into my soul. It's exciting, ecstatic. I can barely keep my cool while Jasik rushes through his bedroom, searching for something.

In an instant, he's pulling open his closet and tearing off his clothes. Blood rushes to my cheeks, and I turn away. Thankfully, I didn't see much more of his naked body than I saw this morning. The last thing I need right now is to be excited *and* aroused.

"We haven't much time," he says, frantic.

I turn to face him. His comfy sweats and T-shirt have been replaced with black jeans, a dark T-shirt, and a military-style jacket. He brushes his hair back when a few strands fall into his eyes.

"Time? For what? What's going on?" I shout.

I remember Malik's words. *Humans have been attacked.* But after that, Jasik was whisking me into his bedroom. I barely got to register his words, let alone ask questions. Obviously something serious has happened, and I ache to know what it is, to be included. I should be next door in my bedroom.

I drop my duffel on the floor and unzip it. I desperately search for my weapon. I find the small black box that contains my cross necklace and push it aside. At the very bottom of the bag, I find the box that secures my stake. I yank it from the bag, open the box, and withdraw my weapon. I stand and kick the bag. It slides against the floor until it knocks into the wall. With stake in hand, I face Jasik.

"I need you to stay here," he says, gaze on the deadly silver in my hand.

"What? But where are you going?" I ask, confused. He is clearly getting ready for a fight. Why would we stay here?

"To aid the humans," he says.

"What humans? What's happening?" I shout. I'm getting angrier by the second.

"Jeremiah was on patrol after breakfast. He must have encountered something and sent word to Malik," he says.

"Sent word? How?" I ask.

"We have cellular telephones, Ava. This is the twenty-first century," Jasik says plainly.

If I wasn't frightened, I might have laughed. Once again, Jasik shows me his softer side. Unfortunately, I can't appreciate it right now.

"Malik, Hikari, and I are going to help him," he says. "You need to stay here."

He turns away from me and faces his dresser. He opens the top drawer, nearly yanking it completely from the furniture, and shuffles inside. By the time he slams it closed and faces me again, he has a dagger in his hand. The silver metal is bright and shiny. The handle is black. He slides it into a hidden sheath inside his inner jacket and strides toward me.

"Why? I should come with you," I argue.

"No. Absolutely not."

"Jasik, I'm an asset. Use me."

"Ava, you're a risk I can't take."

"What's that supposed to mean?" I slide my stake into my jacket's inner pocket and cross my arms over my chest. Rage is building within me, and if he's not careful, I might take it out on him.

"Humans have been attacked. I don't know how many were injured or how many rogues are there. I can't watch you if I'm hunting them."

Jasik tries to pass me, but I sidestep to get in his way. I'm blocking his exit, and I can see his frustration is building.

"You don't need to *watch me*, Jasik. I fed. I'm fine."

"You're an unnecessary risk, and I'm not willing to take the chance. End of discussion."

He swoops around me so fast I completely miss it. I'm facing an empty bedroom and listening to his bedroom door open behind me.

"Why do you even care?" I blurt as I stumble around. I may not be as agile, but I can get the job done.

He stops in his tracks and turns to face me. "Are you seriously asking me that?"

I shrug. "Maybe."

"This attitude and reckless behavior is why you're not

coming and why you *must* train with Malik."

"We don't have time for your power trip, Jasik! I'm coming, and there's nothing you can do to stop me!"

The tiny muscles in his jaw clench. I've overstepped. There will be no going back and no forgiveness before he leaves. He once called me stubborn, and I have to laugh about that now. If I'm stubborn, what is he?

"Ava"—he exhales sharply—"*stay here*." His tone is harsh, and it's pointless to keep arguing.

The door to his bedroom slams shut, and I hear his descending footsteps. With each step, they grow more and more faint. The front door to the manor closes, and I'm alone.

Well, alone as a girl can be when she's in a house full of vampires who don't particularly care for her.

TWELVE

I unlock Jasik's bedroom window and peer down. I'm on the second story of a rather tall Victorian-style manor. I'm not sure how many feet it is until I reach the ground, but it certainly looks to be a higher jump than the one at my old house.

As I shimmy out the window and dangle my legs in the air, I send a silent prayer to whatever god or goddess is listening.

"Time to test these fancy vampire skills," I say aloud.

I'm falling. The air swoops through my hair and tickles my nose. A quick burst of adrenaline rushes through me. Am I flying? I hang my arms out to my sides, as if I really could take off into the night sky, and giggle as I land.

There's no pain, no break, no internal ache. It's as if I've just stepped off a stair or jumped from my bed. The extra height made no difference.

Cautiously, I scan my surroundings. Jasik's bedroom was across the hall from mine, so I've landed in the backyard. The area is unfamiliar yet similar to the front yard. A small clearing leads to overgrown brush and forest trees. The sky is alight with stars that seem brighter ever since I transitioned into a vampire.

There are still several hours before the sun will rise, but I doubt the vampires will need a lot of time. Like me, they're experienced hunters. I'm sure they'll reach the rogues in no time, so I must move quickly if I want to aide them.

I run my hands along the front of my jacket, smoothing down the fabric as I search for my weapon. I need to ensure it hasn't been lost in my escape. If I wish to hunt, I need the tools. I encounter the familiar bulge of my sheathed stake and turn to run toward the front of the manor.

But I stop dead in my tracks.

Amicia stands before me, arms crossed, finger tapping disapprovingly against her bicep. Her eyes are narrowed, her jaw clenched. Her nose is pointed toward the sky as she assesses the situation. She definitely doesn't look amused or pleased to find me jumping out of Jasik's bedroom window.

I'll admit this definitely looks *very* bad. When I arrived unwanted, she made it explicitly clear that she won't tolerate even one mishap. This likely qualifies as that single wrongdoing. I decide to face her head-on, so I swallow the knot that's forming and wait for her to speak.

Except she doesn't.

Time slows to an agonizing pace as I wait for her. Just listening to myself breathe is starting to irk me, and the steady beats of her heart, while mine remains overworked, are just her way of showing off.

I don't have time for this!

I'm not sure how many minutes pass, but the moment it becomes unbearable silence, I finally cave and offer an explanation.

"I can explain," I blurt.

"I'm waiting," she says firmly.

"The other hunters left. I was supposed to catch up with them."

She exhales sharply. "Ava, I'm offering you the chance at

honesty, and you wish to lie to me? Do you take me for a fool?"

I shake my head and break away from her deadly gaze. "No. I just . . . Jasik didn't want me to go with, but I need to."

"And why is that?" Her steely gaze sends shivers down my spine. I don't understand why she affects me this way. She's not my sire, but I'm terrified of her nonetheless. If true strength had a smell, it would smell just like her. A candle company could bottle her up and sell the concoction to witches for lighting during courage rituals. Or skip the ritual. Just light her up and *let it burn*. Inhale deeply and become a new person. Rinse and repeat.

I sigh because the truth is inevitable, so I resort to honesty—not because of what she said but because I'm fairly certain she can actually sense a lie. It's like she has some superpower the rest of us didn't inherit when we transitioned. It also doesn't make sense to keep lying, because she knew I was going to jump out of Jasik's bedroom window enough to wait for me outside; Jasik must have already told her the plan and clued her in to the fact that I wasn't invited.

What a jerk.

"He thinks I'm a liability," I say.

"And you don't agree?"

"No. I have a lot of experience in battle."

She arches a brow. "I'm certain you do. Just how many vampires have you slain, Ava?"

The silence returns, and this time, it's earth-shattering. How am I supposed to answer this question? If I lie, she'll probably sense it and sentence me to death for annoying her— or for my dishonesty. If I tell the truth, she'll hate me, deem me untrustworthy, and cast me out. Either way, I'm basically looking at my last days on earth. It's safe to say this isn't quite how I imagined my final moment with these vampires.

"Amicia, I won't apologize for what I've done, and I don't expect you to answer to me for everything you've done. I'm sure your body count is much higher than mine, and I think we can both agree we did what we had to do."

She nods. "I suppose so."

"I won't deny that I was sneaking out and disobeying Jasik's request to stay here until he returns, but I can't sit by and watch as they face rogues without me. He won't take my word that I'm an asset, so he's forcing me to prove it to him. I can only do that in battle."

"He worries your hunger will get the best of you. How will you control your desire around injured humans?" she asks.

"I think you and I can both agree that I'm the only one in this house who truly cares about protecting humans."

"I resent your accusation. We hunt rogues each and every night." Her tone is sharp, and I worry I've overstepped. Unfortunately, there's no going back now, so I let her have every ounce of my *honesty* that she requested from me.

"You hunt rogues to protect your secret. Vampires don't want to become the dominant species and risk their takeout meals-on-wheels. Extinction means vampires die too. Sure, your actions benefit humans, but that doesn't make them any less selfish. I hunt to protect humans, to keep them safe without expecting anything in return. That has been my sole concern every time I've gone on patrol."

I'm firm, standing my ground, and waiting for Amicia to succumb to my will. I'm *not* going back inside this manor, and the longer she keeps me here, the harder it's going to be for me to track the other vampires. So we need to end this standoff once and for all.

"You judge us for our actions because we benefit from both the elimination of rogues and the protection of humans, but you're overlooking something far greater."

"And what's that?" I say a little too confidently. I doubt there's anything she can say that will prove me wrong.

"*You* are a vampire, Ava."

With everything I have, I want so desperately to argue with her—not about being a vampire. She's right about that. I *am* a vampire, and I need to start acting like one. I must remember that I'll never look at humans the same way again. They aren't docile creatures in need of my protection. They are my source of nutrition.

Thankfully, Amicia doesn't offer me the chance to respond. She exhales slowly and releases some tension, standing straighter and letting her arms dangle at her sides. She strides toward me.

"I admire your resilience, Ava. I hope you prove to be an invaluable asset in my home," she says.

She walks past me, and I turn to keep my gaze on her. She walks through the glass doors that lead to the conservatory and disappears into the manor. Others watch on, their crimson irises like daggers to flesh, but I ignore them and run to the front yard and past the gate.

The moment I'm in the woods, a weight has been lifted from my shoulders. I'm tense in the house, never feeling truly safe or at ease. The vampires will acclimate to my presence, but it'll be a slow venture toward friendship. I hope impressing Amicia will help speed this along. I'd like to sleep with both eyes closed and not fear for my personal belongings.

I clear my mind and try to focus on Jasik. I've spent the most time with him out of all the vampires, so finding him should be fairly simple. I know his mannerisms, the way he thinks, the way he smells. He's a predator in search of his prey, so I don't think he's too worried about covering his own tracks right now. He's no different from the countless vampires I've hunted on my patrols. They never saw me coming either.

I come to a sudden stop. The world is spinning all around me as I try to catch my breath. I have so much strength at my disposal. I feel like I could run for miles without ever tiring. I ache to run until my legs give out just to see how far I'll get. The exhilaration of my new strength and heightened senses is exhausting.

I scan the woods. There are several paths with broken branches. Most come from the wildlife that calls this forest home. I spend several minutes unsuccessfully trying to find Jasik's path. Just when I'm beginning to wonder if all hope is lost, I resort to my final sense.

With nose to the sky like some rabid beast, I inhale deeply. The faint smell of cinnamon reaches my nostrils. I open my eyes and dash toward the smell, risking everything on the hunch that it leads to Jasik and the other vampires. I continue taking several deep inhalations, not worrying about how much noise I must be making as I run toward the familiar smell.

I reach them in a matter of seconds. The three hunters stand in a small grouping on the outskirts of Darkhaven. Jeremiah is still missing. A spark of concern is beginning to burn within me. *Where is he? Has something happened?*

The forest borders Darkhaven on three sides. The vampires built their home within it, hiding so deep in the woods that no one has ever ventured there. We're nowhere near there now.

Clear across the expansive forest, in what some locals

consider the bad side of town, there is Darkhaven's only nightclub, the Catacombs. What was once a prominent church has been converted into a local hangout spot where all the cool kids like to listen to a live band and drink beer smuggled within travel mugs. Since high school kids bring in the greatest revenue, a bouncer sits at the front door to charge a cover, check IDs, and stamp hands.

Even now, from this distance, I can see him. He's a large man wearing a tight tank top that's far too small for his muscular build. His dark skin is slick with sweat. The flickering light above the door reflects off his shiny black curls.

I can hear the live band and distant rumblings of people talking over the music. Every few minutes, the distinct clatter of billiard balls rings through the walls.

The stench is nauseating. The pungent rush of sweat and stale beer is stagnant in the air. I stumble into the clearing, as if I'm drunk from the fumes alone, and make my way toward the vampires. Jasik doesn't hide his annoyance with me.

"I told you she'd sneak out anyway," Hikari says. She doesn't hide her frustration either.

"Jasik, we haven't the time for this," Malik warns.

My sire sighs and turns to face me. "Will you never listen?"

I shrug. "I guess not. Better you learn that now."

"You're a liability," Malik says.

"I'm an ally. You don't have many of those, especially ones already trained to fight rogues, so I suggest you don't piss me off," I say.

Hikari laughs. "Are you seriously threatening him?"

By the time I process her words, she's already in front of me. She's one quick smack away from knocking me unconscious. But I'm brazen, high from the scent of booze and adrenaline.

Before I can respond, Jasik is beside me, separating us as if he really did expect a brawl.

"Ava, you shouldn't have come. You're too great a risk." He turns to face the others. "But we don't have time to escort her back home, so we'll use her."

"Use me? For what?" I say.

"Bait."

The night air is cool against my skin. It's an odd sensation to shiver not from the cold but from uncertainty and fear. I feel the vampires' eyes on me, but I can't distinguish allies from enemies. I have no idea if the vampires stalking me are my nest-mates or rogues on the prowl.

By the time we caught up with Jeremiah, he informed us the humans were already dead. He wasn't able to save them, and I could see from his grim demeanor that he will live with that knowledge the rest of his life. And vampires live *way* too long for that nonsense. It's in these moments I can understand the desire to go rogue, to turn off your emotions and simply act.

He wasn't able to approach the rogues without risking his life. Jasik assured him he made the right decision to wait and call for backup. Their idea of patrolling Darkhaven is so much different than mine. As a witch, I was expected to kill any vampire I encountered. No one cared about my safety. No one thought to have me call for help first. No one ever offered to join me.

The vampires truly care for each other. They may not be

blood relatives, but they are *family*. They're nothing like what the witches taught me to believe. *What else have they lied about?*

The vampires and I have split up in search of the rogues. We're all within earshot, and I feel like they're expecting me to mess up so badly the rogues find me first.

Hence, *bait*.

But I intend to prove them wrong. I will find a rogue and kill it before the others even realize what's going on. Then, maybe I'll get the respect I so rightfully deserve.

Just as I'm developing my plan, something happens. It's a distinct moment in time, like when the wind shifts or the temperature drops suddenly, and it leaves me on edge. My pulse races, my heart pounding so loudly it's all I can think about. My senses rapid-fire. The smell, the sounds, the lights . . . they all become too much. I want to cower and fight at the same time.

I home in on a girl, maybe seven or eight. She's far too young to be outside alone this late at night. The moonlight dances for the dead, not the living. If the rogues find her, it wouldn't take much to end her existence completely. Her parents will wake tomorrow and wonder what happened to their bright ray of sunshine, and they'll never know. They'll never find out. She will simply be *gone*.

I rush to her, reaching her side at the same time I hear the familiar growl of an approaching rogue. I turn to face him. The deadly vampire smiles at me, flashing inch-long fangs already tainted pink by someone else's blood. He runs toward me, and I cannot move. I'm frozen in place, simultaneously mesmerized by my attacker and traumatized by my last encounter with a rogue.

His black leather pants are shiny and make a cracking sound every time he takes a step toward me. His fishnet mesh top is too tight, clinging to his thin torso as if it were an extra layer of skin. His striking short hair is over-gelled and dyed neon red. It points straight to the sky on all sides. But nothing compares to the hunger I see in his crimson eyes. It stops me in my tracks and leaves me breathless.

The moment he reaches me, I remember why I'm here and why I fight for them. Too weak to save themselves, humans need a hero.

I spin to face the girl and push her backward so she'll remain out of the rogue's reach. By the time I turn back around to face the monster, he's already in front of me. He wraps his thin, bony fingers around my neck and tosses me aside like I'm a sack of garbage being taken out.

I slam against the brick wall of the Catacombs and slide down the rigid stone until I crumple into a heap on the dirty alley street. I fall to my knees and try to push myself up. Shards of broken beer bottles dig into my palms, cutting my skin. I wince and hold my hands up to assess the damage. Already, my skin is beginning to heal over.

I rip out a jagged edge and crawl to my feet. My entire body aches from the impact of one *hangry* rogue. I wipe off the glass that clings to my jeans and glance up in time to brush noses with the short but deadly vampire.

In the distance, the girl is crying. I ignore her because I figure if the rogue is focusing on me, then she should be fine. I want to tell her it'll be okay and not to be scared. I want to tell her she'll be home soon enough, but the moment the rogue's hand slams against my chest, I can't speak. I can't breathe. I can only listen to the internal protests of my sternum breaking.

I gasp so loudly I'm sure I'll attract attention. If the vampires didn't know I was in danger before, they certainly do now. Every ounce of air exits my lungs in a quick, painful burst. I try to gasp for more, but the rogue's fingers are at my neck again. I claw at his hands, breaking skin, but this only amuses him. In addition to turning off his ability to empathize, he must not be able to feel much pain. Or maybe he's a sick freak who relishes in the fulfillment of torture.

In my last desperate attempt to save myself, I reach for my hidden stake. I pull it free quickly and easily thanks to all the years of training the witches forced upon me.

I'm flush against the grimy walls. Something slick tickles the back of my hand as I try to wedge the stake against the rogue's chest so I can thrust it forward. But there's no room. My chest burns from lack of oxygen, and my limbs feel heavy.

The rogue says something and laughs, but I can't hear him. All I can hear is the desperate pleas from my lungs and the constant drum of my heart in my head.

The rogue squeezes my neck harder, and I lose the ability to maintain my hold on the stake. It falls from my grasp, and I wait for the distinct clatter of failure as it hits the ground.

Except it never comes.

In some twisted sense of luck, the rogue caught the stake with his free hand. He thrusts it forward and plunges it into my chest.

I gasp as the metal pierces my skin and breaks through bone. I want to scream or cry or, heck, even beg for mercy. But I can't do any of those things. I can only wait for my inevitable demise, for the darkness to wash over me like a warm blanket, for eternal peace.

The rogue laughs, and I realize he's staked the wrong side.

He finds pleasure in torturing me. Just as he's about to plunge it into my chest again, he stops. His grip loosens, and his eyes nearly bulge from their sockets. After just a few seconds, he turns to dust.

I'm falling, and this time, I never hit the ground.

I fall against my savior, gasping for air. My lungs burn at the intrusion. The cool air is like fire in my chest, but I can't stop. I continue to gasp until my racing heart slows and my vision clears.

Someone is speaking to me, telling me I'm okay now.

I open my eyes, expecting to find Jasik comforting me, only to see Hikari. She's wrapped her arms around me, pulling me close to her. She scans our surroundings while holding my limp body in her lap.

The soft footsteps of approaching vampires grows louder.

"Help the girl!" Hikari shouts. "I've got Ava."

She rubs loose strands of hair from my eyes. I keep my gaze focused on her, mimicking her breathing, her steady heartbeat.

"Can you stand?" she asks.

I nod. My head is still spinning, but I already feel a million times better.

Hikari helps me up, and I lean into her. She supports me and rubs her hand up and down my back as I rest against her solid frame.

"You're okay," she says.

We take several steps away from the wall. The ground is crunchy beneath my feet as I try to maneuver around garbage and filth.

A soft amber light from an overhang illuminates the alley, and we step under it. I nod at Hikari that I'm okay, and she hands me my stake before stepping aside.

Gripping my chest, I search for the girl. My stomach twists as I try to comprehend the scene before me. Jasik's bloody wrist is pushed against the girl's mouth, and she's drinking his blood. The girl's gaze darts around the alleyway until it finally settles on me.

"What are you doing to her?" I shout as I stumble forward.

"Ava, stop!" Hikari shouts.

I blink, and Malik is no longer by Jasik's side. He's in front of me and preventing me from reaching his brother.

"Get out of my way," I say, seething.

"He's saving her life—something that wouldn't have been necessary if you had listened to him in the first place," Malik argues.

"What? What are you talking about? The rogue didn't even touch her," I say.

"No, but you did, didn't you?" Malik asks.

I gasp, furious by the accusation. "I *never* fed from her!"

"Feeding isn't the only way to hurt a human, Ava," Hikari says.

Malik steps aside so I can watch what Jasik is doing. The girl's arms are bloody with slashes, and her T-shirt is stained. Her pants are soaked in urine, and her cheeks are streaked from tears.

I cover my shock with my hands. "I—I didn't mean to."

"You're stronger than you realize right now," Malik says.

"Will she be okay?" I ask.

Jasik nods, his eyes searching mine. I'm not sure what I see in them. Anger? Understanding? Fear?

"He's healing her," Hikari explains.

"Will she..." I trail off. I can't bring myself to say the

words. This is a child! Spending eternity as a preteen would be torture.

"No. Transitioning is a complicated process. His blood will heal her and work its way out of her system within a day or so," Malik says.

I sheath my stake and take a seat beside the little girl. I don't care that I'm sitting in filth or that I nearly died. My only concern is for this child who now fights for her life because I pushed her so hard she flew through the air like a damn superhero.

"I'm sorry," I whisper, but it's too late. The damage has been done. The girl was attacked by a vampire, and she witnessed the whole thing.

THIRTEEN

Something about the forest feels different. It's like the trees, the flowers, and the creatures that hide here know my secret. They witnessed my failure, and they're mocking me— even the way the moonlight cascades through the branches is insulting. I wrap my arms around my chest and stare into the distance.

Jeremiah is carrying the girl toward the bouncer. The man stops counting the large wad of cash he's handling from taking cover charges and looks up. He stands so quickly, the stool he was sitting on falls over, hitting the ground in a loud smack. The door to the club is open, but the partygoers don't even notice the commotion outside.

Earlier, we all agreed that a group of strangers carrying her into the club would look too suspicious, so Jeremiah volunteered to be the decoy. He feigns horror as he rushes toward the security guard.

"I found her in the alley behind the club!" he shouts. He carefully offers just enough shock and outrage to convince the man he had nothing to do with it.

"Bring her inside!" the man yells, even though Jeremiah is now right beside him.

Jeremiah nods so frantically, the hood on his sweatshirt bobs up and down.

"You got her?" the bouncer questions. He scans Jeremiah's physique. Jeremiah may not be as ripped as the bouncer, but he's definitely in shape. Obviously the man in the small tank top can't seem to look past Jeremiah's sweatshirt.

"Yeah. Come on. She might be hurt," Jeremiah says.

They rush inside, and from our rendezvous point in the forest, I can no longer see what happens, but I hear everything. A girl near the door screams. The singer stops singing, but the band doesn't follow his lead until a few seconds later. Finally, the drummer ceases his solo debut.

"Lay her down here!" someone shouts, and a clattering of glasses smash against the floor.

"Someone call the police," the bouncer yells before asking the girl if she's okay. She doesn't respond. He asks if someone hurt her, and again she doesn't respond.

I didn't realize how tense I was until Jasik places his hand over my own. I'd practically clawed my way through the arm of my jacket.

Several different sets of beeps echo throughout the building. I imagine the dispatcher will be receiving *a lot* of calls tonight.

I close my eyes and listen more intently.

"9-1-1, what is your emergency?" a woman asks.

"Yes, there's a girl. A child. I think she's hurt," someone else says.

I open my eyes and search for Jasik's. He's watching me closely. Is he as nervous as I am? I can't tell. His usual calm demeanor gives away nothing tonight.

"What if she tells them what happened?" I ask. After all, she *did* see us. She knows our faces, and worst of all, she knows *what we are.*

147

"She won't," Jasik replies. He seems certain, but I'm not.

"How can you be so sure?" I ask.

"This isn't the first time we've saved a witness," he says.

"And they never tell?" I ask.

"They might, but nothing ever comes of it. I suppose those who speak up aren't believed," he says.

I nod. He's right. If I were human and a mother, I wouldn't believe my child if she told me she was hurt—and then saved—by a vampire. I'd have her see a therapist, which is exactly what this girl needs after tonight.

The distant sounds of approaching sirens blare through the village. With each passing second, they grow louder and louder until they're almost unbearable.

I glance down the street. Blue-and-red lights dance across buildings as they approach. I look up to the moon to try to assess the hour. The police have arrived at the club in record time. Although, in a small village like Darkhaven, they were probably itching for something to do. It sucks that it had to be this.

The squad cars come to a screeching halt. The noise ceases, but the lights remain flashing as two officers open the doors and run into the building. Onlookers shout. It's hard to hear because everyone is talking at once. The police shout for them to be quiet. They want to see the girl.

In the chaos, Jeremiah slips out. He's by our side so quickly, I'm sure they don't even realize he's missing.

"Is she okay?" I ask Jeremiah.

He nods. "She's going to be fine. They'll make sure she gets home."

I'm happy she's safe, but my heart aches for the girl. I can only imagine what her home life must be like if she was able to escape into the night. I hope she gets help. I hope the police look into the situation and make sure it doesn't happen again. Tonight, she was lucky. Tomorrow, she could be dead.

"Everything is going to be okay, Ava," Jasik says. His words are reassuring. Suddenly, the forest no longer plots against me. I'm stronger and more confident in my actions, even if I was just questioning everything I did tonight.

Malik exhales sharply. "No, it's not."

"Malik," Jasik says, his tone sharp. "Don't."

"I must, brother," he says before turning to face me head-on. I swallow as the vampire stares me down. "Your pride is a nuisance. You need to stop this nonsense and embrace what you are, what you've become. You're *not* a witch anymore, Ava. You must train, or you are going to get someone killed."

I don't say anything—at least, not right away. He's right. Tonight proves that. I am a liability. I'm not looking forward to admitting I've been stubborn about this.

"You cannot hunt with us if you are going to risk our lives," Malik continues.

"Malik, stop—"

"No, he's right," I interrupt Jasik. "I almost killed a girl, a *child*, and I almost died in the process. If the rogue had been paying attention to his surroundings, Hikari might have been injured—or worse. And she was trying to *save* me." I shake my head, trying not to think about the road not taken.

"You will train with me?" Malik asks, although I'm not quite sure if he's actually asking me or if he's telling me I have no choice.

"I will," I say.

"We will begin immediately," he says.

I nod, but Malik is already walking away. Jeremiah joins

him, and I'm left with Hikari and Jasik.

"Hikari—"

"Don't," she interrupts.

"But—"

"I don't need you to thank me for doing my job," she says.

"And yet, I still want to."

She smiles. "You're welcome."

"Can I ask you something?"

She shrugs but doesn't object. I'm sure she knows what I'm about to say.

"Why did you save me instead of the girl?"

"You would have died. The girl was fine."

"Right. It's not like she needed blood to heal or anything..." I arch a brow, silently telling her I need a better answer than what she's given me.

She exhales slowly. "Look, I don't particularly like you, and I certainly don't trust you, but I don't exactly dislike you."

"Um...okay?" I say, confused. I'm way too tired to follow that logic.

"Jasik sired you. Whether I like it or not, you're family," she explains.

When Hikari went through my bedroom and completely invaded my privacy, she did it because of her loyalty to her family. She was sure I was a threat, and she did what she felt she had to do to oust me. Not only can I respect that, I can relate to it. I would have done the same if a vampire-turned-witch showed up at my coven and asked for refuge. At the very least, I'd make sure the person wasn't a threat.

"Well, thanks for saving my life," I say.

"Sure. Don't mention it," she says before running to catch up with the others.

I turn to Jasik. "So what happens now?"

"What do you mean?"

"Amicia gave me one chance. Is she going to boot me for this?"

He smiles. "I'll talk to her. Maybe she hasn't even noticed you left."

I gnaw on my lower lip. "Yeah, about that . . ."

We're only a few miles from home when a familiar sensation returns. It's like something inside me is screaming to be released. There's a spark in my gut that's threatening to flame. My nerves rapid-fire, and a chill courses through my veins, turning my blood into ice.

It feels like someone is watching me.

Am I the only one who feels this way? The other vampires don't seem to be acting any differently. Do they not sense incoming danger? Am I making something out of nothing?

"Jasik?" I say.

He glances at me, and the world falls into darkness. A piercing throb erupts within my skull. I worry my brain might actually burst.

I cry out, shrieking for Jasik, for anyone. My eyes are closed. I can't open them without the pain intensifying, so I remain in the dark.

I grapple on the ground and dig my fingers into loose soil. Slowly, as the pain begins to dull and the screaming within my head softens to a whisper, I am able to hear the chaos exploding all around me.

Someone is shouting for me, urging me to stand, to move,

to fight. I mumble something incoherent even to me. More shouts, and I open my eyes.

The light is blinding—so much so, I snap my eyelids shut again. I reach for the back of my head and rub the spot that hurts and wince the moment hand meets flesh. At the base of my skull, my hair is wet. I bring my hand forward and chance a peek. My hand is coated in blood. *My blood*. What the heck is happening?

I try to sit up, but I'm hit by a wave of nausea and fall over, nearly heaving my breakfast. I roll onto my back and open my eyes. The moon welcomes me. She's still big and beautiful like she was the night of the full moon. As she begins to wane, she's not quite as round anymore, but she's responsive nonetheless.

I reach for her. I could never touch her, but I can use her power. I can try to tap into it, into the earth, and use it to heal me. At least, I could if I were still a witch.

Someone stands over me, blocking my view of the moon. Moonlight shines brightly behind the figure, distorting my vision so I can't clearly see who it is.

"Jasik?" I whisper. My head is throbbing. I wince when I try to see him better and only succeed in scraping my wound against the hard-packed ground.

The voice that escapes my throat doesn't sound like my own. It's weak; it breaks. I need to be stronger than this. I need to survive. I didn't risk becoming a vampire just so I could die here tonight.

The figure steps to the side, and I first notice a familiar set of crimson irises. A tall vampire hovers over me. His broad shoulders make it hard to see anything but his overly muscular body.

His cold eyes contrast against his dark skin. He's confident as he smiles down at me. I remember his shaved head, his smooth skin, and his long, deadly fangs. I remember the pain when they pierced my untouched neck. It was earth-shattering and shook me to my core.

This is him. The vampire who stole my life, who attacked my coven, who killed my friends. He stands before me as if he has no worry in the world.

Maybe it's time I give him one.

"Hello, Ava," he says.

I thrust my legs upward, striking him between the legs. He stumbles backward, cursing. I repeat the move, this time hitting him in the torso. He falls backward. One final time, I thrust my weight onto my arms and pounce upward so I now stand while he lies on the ground.

He laughs a hearty full bellow. "I'm impressed."

He mirrors my move and effortlessly propels himself forward so he can jump to his feet.

"Ava!"

Jasik shouts for me, and I can hear everything he's begging of me from that one word. He wants me to be careful, to come to the others for aid, but I am blinded by my hatred and in desperate need of revenge.

I'm overrun with blood-soaked vengeance. My head aches, but I don't care. I'm not even worried if the injury is deadly—so long as I can bring my new friend with me.

The weight of my stake tucked safely in the confines of my jacket is comforting. Over the course of my long career in hunting vampires, I've perfected the ability to pull it out and use it faster than even a vampire's heightened senses can keep up with my movements. The stake was my only defense against the vampires.

Sometimes I won because I was better. Other times I won because vampires are too cocky. Occasionally it was just blind luck on my side. But tonight, I will win because this debt is owed to me. I've spent my life protecting the earth, and it's time Mother Nature pays her dues.

"Do you know what I like about you?" the rogue vampire asks.

"Is it my sparkling personality?" I respond.

He smiles. "I do appreciate your wit, but it's your drive that appeals to me. Even when everything is against you, you stubbornly proceed. You charge, full force and without brains, toward your desire. You simply won't allow yourself to fail. Even now, you don't care about your friends. You only care about your revenge." He speaks slowly, emphasizing each word. They wrap around me, cocooning me, suffocating me. He's right. I haven't even considered how my nest-mates are faring.

I tear my gaze from the vampire and search for my friends. Desperately, they fight against other rogues. Jasik and the others are severely outnumbered and dangerously distracted . . . *by me*. If only I'd stayed inside and obeyed his request. None of this would have happened. I wouldn't have injured the girl, nearly died, or risked Hikari's life. I wouldn't be here, and the rogues might not have attacked. After all, their leader is making it pretty clear his only interest is for me.

Jasik and I make eye contact, but our exchange is brief. The sorrow in his eyes is almost too much to bear. I tear away from his gaze and turn to refocus on the rogue.

It's just *one* vampire.

Vampire versus vampire.

I can do this. I can win.

I turn my back on my friends to find my enemy, except he's gone. I spin in circles until I'm dizzy, but I don't spot him. Where could he have gone? In the midst of a war, he retreats? Why do that? Why come all this way and plan this entire fight, just to leave?

"We end this tonight!" I shout.

My threat doesn't faze the vampires or rogues. The clatter of metal striking metal still rings in my head and echoes in the air all around us. No one has stopped to consider my words, to aid or fight me. They continue on, and they're in need of my help.

Twigs break under weight in the distance, and I turn to face the noise. My stomach grows uneasy, making it nearly impossible to focus on the sound in the woods.

Though I can't see him—*yet*—I know he's there, watching, waiting. Slowly, I take a step toward the sound. My gaze sweeps the woods, but I see nothing except forest.

I release several deep breaths, trying to steady my overworked heart. I need this rogue to consider me a threat, a predator. I am *not* his prey—not anymore. He may have retreated, but I would follow him to the ends of the earth. I promise myself he will meet an untimely death at the hands of my stake—the very weapon that should have ended his existence the moment we met in the cemetery a few days ago.

I refuse to back down. After all, killing the monster who ruined my life is good practice and will prove to the vampires that I'm worthy of training. They'll consider me an ally, an asset.

I stand tall, threateningly. My hands are clenched at my sides. My fangs lengthen as I release a long-awaited deep growl. I imagine sinking my fangs into his neck and drinking him dry. I pretend he's a shriveled corpse before me. I stake him. If only it were that easy.

Three rogues emerge past the tree line. They are strong, old. I sense their strength the moment they appear. Just like when I'm around Amicia, something within me screams, but I have no interest in pleasing them the way I wish to please her. After all, they have no link to Jasik. I'm beginning to realize older vampires emit a powerful scent. They smell like ash and blood.

The rogues approaching me wear bloodstained clothes, and their skin is caked with dirt. As I assess their physique— and the mathematic probability of my survival rate—they continue approaching me. They walk with confidence that shakes me to my core.

"I have no interest in fighting your patsies. This is between you and me," I shout, hoping the rogue will take the bait.

Unfortunately he doesn't.

I curse under my breath and prepare myself for one heck of a fight.

The tallest of the three charges me first, and I remind myself that I will stand my ground. I will not falter. If it comes down to death, I accept that fate. Dying to protect myself and those who care about me is a good way to go.

The rogue approaches me from the front. A fatal mistake. I'm smaller and more agile than this beast.

I lunge forward just as he is within arm's reach. I twist to the side and spin around until I stand behind him. I pounce on his back, wrapping my legs around his waist. He grumbles something inaudible, but I ignore him. I'm too busy grabbing his head and jerking it to the side as hard as I can.

With my fingers knotted in his hair, his neck snaps. We

fall to the ground. Still on top of him, I dig my knee into his back. The other is firmly planted against the ground. Snapping his neck won't kill him, so I need to make a permanent move before the other vampires reach my side.

Scraping my nails against his scalp, I pull his head upward by his hair while pushing his torso down with my knee. His head detaches swiftly, and I somersault away and face my attackers.

But the other two vampires haven't yet approached. They stand, jaws ajar in disbelief. I lift my bloody souvenir in the air, displaying the vampire's head. I toss it toward them, but it bursts into ash before it reaches their feet.

I take their moment of uncertainty for my advantage. I raise my arms to my sides, my fingers flicking them toward me in a daring move. I arch a brow.

"Well, boys. Let's dance," I say, smiling.

The larger of the two growls. His muscles tighten as he throws his arms out to his sides and curls his fingers into fists. He runs toward me, his feet smacking the ground with each step, sending shock waves through the earth. He slams into me, and I fly through the air. I crash into a tree, its branch piercing my gut. I cry out and stare at the protruding limb. It's coated in my blood. I'm not sure how much more I can lose before I must feed.

I gasp for air and grab on to the branch. Every second it is inside me is excruciating.

I rest the soles of my feet against the rough bark of the thick trunk. Pushing against the tree, I begin to slide off at an agonizing pace.

Before I can free myself, the other vampire reaches me. He grabs on to my arms and yanks me forward. I scream as the branch scrapes against flesh and bone. With the tree no longer holding my weight, I fall to the ground in a heap.

The vampire is beside me, and I'm too weak to stand. He grabs me by the neck and lifts me in the air until my legs dangle beneath me. I kick, trying to jab him at the perfect angle to release me, to no avail.

He pushes me up against the tree and slams my skull against the trunk once, twice, three times. I see stars and cease fighting. My limbs dangle lifelessly at my sides.

"*Incendia*," I choke, trying to summon spirit magic.

But nothing happens.

Fire does not aid me—not anymore. I'm weak, and I've lost my magic. Vampire against vampire is too fair a fight. I need an edge if I want to win.

The vampire leans into me, and I thrust my arms upward, striking him between his forearms and jabbing him in the chin. Disoriented, he releases me. I land on my feet and punch him in the chest. My fist breaks through bone, sliding right through his heart.

He wails the moment his heart is shredded, like meat to claws. I grab on to the remains and yank them free. He turns to dust, and I set my sights on the final rogue vampire.

I'm exhausted, but I must fight if I ever want to aid my friends and return home.

He rushes toward me, and I stumble backward until I'm flush against the tree. I risk a daring move. Reaching for a low-hanging branch, I snap it off and spin it in my hand before chucking it at my attacker. He grunts, nearly rolling his eyes, at my fruitless maneuver.

He grabs the branch before it even comes close to his chest, and with a squeeze of his hand, it crumbles into pieces.

He howls, heaving from impact. His skin pales, his eyes widen. He's flying through the air and slams into the ground before turning to dust like the rest of them.

I smile. I was counting on his confidence. While he was focused on my distraction, my stake was slicing through the air at record speed. It flew past the broken bits of branch that were falling from his grasp and plunged into his chest with such velocity, it flung him backward.

Now he's nothing but dust.

Waiting for my next formidable attacker, I limp toward my weapon, pick it up, and grip it tightly.

"I said," I shout, breathing heavily, "we're finishing this!"

A hand rests against my shoulder, and I spin around frantically, flinging my stake toward the intruder as if it's a machete capable of hacking away flesh. I bring it down, and something catches my arm midair.

Jasik stands beside me, eyes wide. His forehead is slick from sweat, his skin caked with dirt. His clothes are torn and blood-soaked. I yank my arm away and fall against him. He wraps his arms around me, and we embrace as if we're the only two vampires remaining.

I can't explain the way I feel, knowing he survived. I'm not sure I even want to understand it. For now, I'm grateful he made it through the mess of rogues preventing him from reaching my side.

"It was a trap," I say. My voice is muffled by Jasik's jacket, but he nods, brushing against the crown of my head. We sit like this for a moment until our pulses sync and my worries fade.

Finally, we pull away, and I search for our allies. Though they all survived, it's clear their strength has been depleted as well. We remain victorious, having eliminated the small army of rogues sent to destroy them and test me. They may be gone, but one still lives.

I face the woods. I feel his gaze lingering on me, and I'm sure his lips have twisted into a sly smile. Having defeated his warriors, I suppose I've passed his test, and that can only mean one thing.

He'll return for me, and we'll end this once and for all.

FOURTEEN

The basement training quarters aren't what I was expecting. Even though the basement beautifully matches the manor's Gothic decor, I still expected a basement out of a horror film: gloomy, concrete floors, goo-covered walls, broken windows, dead bodies sprawled about. The usual stuff you see in vampire horror flicks.

Wall sconces provide minimal lighting in the tight and winding hallway, but my eyes adjust quickly. It takes only seconds for the shadows to dissipate. We pass a few doors as we approach the end of the hallway.

"What's down here?" I ask, generally curious.

"The armory, our training room, storage, and such."

I raise a brow at the armory part. They have an actual armory? That tidbit would have been useful to know a couple of days ago when the rogues attacked.

"Believe it or not," Jasik continues, "we don't simply awaken with the skills needed to kill. We train to use these weapons."

"Of course not. That would be too easy." Internally, I curse the fact that we can't just be naturally good at things. I need an edge.

The large training room is behind the second-to-last door. The wall to the left of the entrance is floor-to-ceiling mirrors.

The wall adjacent to the mirrors is full of weapons: crossbows, spears, blades. The carpeted floor in the hallway doesn't continue into the room. Instead, the entire flooring is matted with a foam floor tile. Gently, I push my heels into it, testing its plushness. There isn't any fancy workout equipment. There is just padded flooring and a wall of weapons.

Something shiny and silver catches my eye. I walk over to the wall and slide my fingers across the blade. I'm not sure what it is. Having a curved tip and between two to three feet long, it seems too curved to be a sword, too thick to be a katana, and too long to be a dagger. But it sure is pretty. The end of the mirrored blade is cased in a black handle with swirling silver lines that glisten in the light. The tip of the handle has a metallic stone. I rub my finger over the smooth surface. I pull the weapon from the wall, my palm firmly grasping it in place.

Jasik steps behind me, placing a hand atop my own, and turns the blade. "Hold it like this," he says.

I am painfully aware of his proximity. His breath is cool on the back of my neck. I turn my head and meet his gaze, letting his fingers linger against my own. His skin lightly brushes against mine, and I shiver as something sparks inside me.

I say nothing—afraid to break the moment, yet terrified to let it continue.

How does he have such sway over me? But more importantly, why do I keep letting it happen? As if reading my thoughts, he pulls away, clearing his throat.

"That's a Celtic seax," he says. He turns his back to me and fiddles with something atop the table positioned directly across from the wall of weapons. "The handle has a very powerful crystal: hematite. It's believed that hematite protects warriors in battle, so this particular stone holds great value to hunters. I've had it since I was a child. It was my father's." He turns to face me, holding a small dagger, swirling it around in his hand while he speaks. "It's been restored, and if you like it, I want you to have it," he says.

"What? No. I can't. It's a family heirloom. I couldn't take this," I say.

He chuckles. "I suppose it is, but no one has used it for quite some time. I'd rather have it be of use than collecting dust."

I look at the blade, raising it and resting the tip on my free palm. I move my arms up and down, testing its weight. It does feel good in my hands.

I nod. "Okay. I mean, if you're sure. It would be nice to have something else." I plan to keep my stake, but after my last fight, having a weapon only effective in hand-to-hand combat is troubling. This will help me kill more efficiently. Slice and dice is the way to go when I'm staring down several sets of crimson eyes.

"Great, and I have a scabbard for it," Jasik says, setting down the dagger and walking across the room to a cabinet.

A scabbard?

"I made this to fit on my back." He opens the cabinet door and grabs what I assume is the scabbard. "You'll need to practice sliding the blade in and out of the sheath, but in time, you will wield this weapon as effectively as you use your stake."

He tightens the arms on the scabbard to accommodate my smaller frame and tells me to turn around. I set the seax on the table and slide my arms into the loopholes. It wears like gun holsters in a Wild West movie, and it fits as if it were meant for me. This seals the deal. I'm definitely taking this weapon with me during my more dangerous patrols.

I step away from Jasik and admire myself in the mirrors, turning my head to the side, trying to see how the scabbard rests against my back. It looks good and lies flat. If I needed to conceal it, it shouldn't be too noticeable beneath a jacket.

I grab the seax from the table and mimic Jasik's swirly maneuver, which is easier than I anticipated with such a large weapon. I am used to twirling smaller weapons, like my stake, but the weight of a seax handles differently. It's much more manageable than I anticipated. I could get used to this.

Feeling daring, I flip the blade upward in a twirling motion before yanking it down, hoping my aim will come as quickly and easily as my weapon-twirling. The seax slides into its sheath like it was waiting for this very moment all those years it was cooped up in this dank, dusty basement.

I face Jasik, smiling from ear to ear, but his pale face makes me frown.

"What is it?" I ask.

"You nearly gave me a heart attack! You must learn and train properly to wield a weapon of this magnitude. You can't just swing it around and hope for the best."

"Okay, sorry," I say, a little more forcefully than intended.

"You could have died, Ava. One miscalculation, and that blade would have sliced through your torso. You can't heal from being chopped in half," he says dryly.

"I know. You're right. I was just excited. I wasn't thinking," I say.

He nods and offers me a small smile. "You should prepare. Malik will be here any minute, and he takes training seriously."

"Is that why he's training me and you're not?" I ask.

He shrugs. "He's the better trainer for you."

"And why is that?" I ask.

Jasik is silent for a moment. "He feels no temptation."

I swallow hard and whisper, "And you do?"

"I'm your sire, Ava. I will always feel something for you."

The palm of his hand finds the center of my chest in a quick jab. I am propelled backward. I hit the brick wall with a force that pushes the air out of my lungs. Chunks of brick fall beside me, a cloud of dust coating the air. I push myself off the ground, the bones in my chest slowly healing from my brush with death.

As I stand, my fangs lower, and instinctively I take a predatory stance.

"Good, but you must immediately counterattack, Ava," Malik says.

I brush off my hands and roll my eyes. "Yeah, yeah. I know." My fangs retract, and I kick the pieces of stone at my feet.

"This is important. They came for you once, and they will come again. He will stop at nothing to claim you."

"Thanks for reminding me there's a big evil out there, and he only wants to play with me," I say sarcastically.

I cross my arms over my chest as if his words don't bother me. I pretend I'm not worried, but it's a lie. I know Malik can sense my growing nervousness and my fear, but I still try to hide it. I need everyone to believe I am as strong as they are.

"You must be ready for any attack," he says.

"I am," I argue, annoyed with his accusation. I started preparing to fight vampires while I was still a child. Dying at the hands of one hasn't changed that.

I blink, and he dashes to the other side of the room. He grabs the dagger Jasik was playing with earlier, spins it around, and throws it. It slices through the air, flying past my face with precision accuracy. Only centimeters from slicing my cheek, it seems to move in slow motion. I reach forward, grab on to the weapon by the tip of the blade, and throw it back. I don't miss my target. The thin blade plants itself in the center of a bull's eye on the back wall.

Malik smiles. "Impressive."

I nod. Heck, even I'm happy with my reflexes. They're better than I thought they'd be after my fight with the rogues. I thought I'd be healing from those injuries for weeks.

"You are well-trained, Ava," Malik says.

"I am. I was a hunter too," I say proudly.

I hope my enthusiasm will give him more confidence in me. I want him to see me as a member of his team, not as Jasik's mistake. I held my own against three rogue vampires, and I emerged victorious. After that, Malik *has* to trust me to join the ranks and help patrol.

Instead, Malik frowns, and I fear I've crossed a line. I probably shouldn't tell a vampire that I'm experienced in hunting his kind, especially if I happen to be sparring with said vampire.

After a few seconds, he finally responds. "Your past will be an asset."

"I think so. I've trained for years. You just need to trust that I'm ready for this."

FIFTEEN

I watch them from afar, never stepping too close, never getting in their crosshairs. I know how dangerous they can be—even to me.

They don't know I'm here, watching, waiting, lurking in the shadows like a true night stalker. They don't know they're a blink away from their greatest enemy . . . me.

It's been one month since I died . . . and was reborn. So much has happened in the last thirty days. So much has changed.

They walk into the backyard in a single-file line, and I think about how familiar everything feels. Sage is burning, and the smell wafts through the air, tickling my heightened senses. Fighting a sneeze, I scrunch my nose. The burning herb bundles are irritating.

Dozens of candles burn brightly, distorting the scene before me. They're too bright for my tired eyes, so I move to hide behind a different tree—one that doesn't block my view of them but covers the candles that are scattered around the ground. They never even see me.

Everything they do, they do in unison. It's clear they've been practicing this for years. Decades, even. Their technique is flawless, and they all work so well together. It reminds me of home.

The other vampire hunters and I have succumbed to a comfortable rhythm too. Gone are the days of petty arguments and baseless accusations. We get along fairly well when tempers aren't flared. I even embark on my own hunts now, but those are rare.

Tonight is one of the few times I'm allowed to hunt alone. Jasik doesn't trust me. I think it's because he doesn't understand my appreciation for the shadows, for the hunt, for the *kill*. He says it's because I'm not ready yet. I'm not as strong as he believes I can be. He tells me I'm special. A witch-turned-vampire is a rare creature, and I need to test my strength, my power, my endurance. To make him happy—and secretly because I kind of love sparring—I train with Malik as often as he can handle me.

Malik doesn't appreciate my sense of humor, and I don't appreciate his lack of one. Whenever I get on his nerves, which is fairly often, he likes to hurt my feelings by telling me he only tolerates me staying at the manor because I'll be homeless if I'm voted out—as if we're on some reality television show. I don't let him know how much his words actually do hurt. He's right. I would be homeless.

I'm building trust with my new vampire family—I think even Amicia is starting to like having me around—but I'll never forget my first home. I'll never forget the witches who brought me into this world and then forced me out.

Instead of taking the high road and ignoring his comments, I like to mention Malik's new mystery woman. He hates when I bring her up, so we pretty much talk about her every day. I ask him when he'll bring her to the manor, and he tells me he never will. I ask what's wrong with her, and he tells me she's perfect. I tell him I'll break down his walls eventually, and he tells me I have my own romance to worry about.

Around this time, my cheeks burn, and I call off the sparring match. For some reason, I just can't talk about Jasik in front of Malik. I assure Malik nothing is going on as I'm practically tripping over my own feet to get away from him. Clearly I'm stealthy and incredibly agile, and I don't know why they don't trust me to patrol on my own more often ...

The witches I'm spying on are shouting something now. I move closer. All that separates us is one line of small trees and several feet of open space. I imagine this is where the rogues were hiding the day they came for my soul.

I listen to the witches and try not to be seen because I'm not quite sure how I'd explain myself to them or the vampires.

I scan their familiar faces in search of the one I seek. It doesn't take long to find her. She looks just like me, except several worry lines crease her aging skin. I can't remember if those were there before or if they're new. It's been so long since I've seen her. She looks the same, yet different. Would I look the same to her? Maybe if I step out and show her I'm here ...

I shake my head, trying to clear my thoughts. Of course, this never works, but Jasik insists I have a chaperon because I'm reckless. I'm trying to prove to him I won't do something stupid just because I'm alone.

Sometimes it's hard to be in the manor with him there. When I'm not sneaking around trying to discover the identity of Malik's new girlfriend or begging him to spar, I'm fighting my ever-growing and oh-so-annoying attraction for Jasik. It's a daily battle. The fact that he feels the same way makes it that much harder.

The witches stand in a circle, interlocking hands to form one united front. They stare at the sky, and the moon shines down upon them. They bless the moon and thank her for her radiance over the past month.

At the center of the circle of witches, there is an altar cluttered with keepsakes and ritual relics. There's something for every element and a sphere to represent the moon. Beside it, glistening as the moonlight gleams upon it, there is a silver cross. It's an exact replica of the cross Papá gave me. I don't know if it's Mamá's or if she had it made after I left.

I sigh and glance down. My neck is bare. My silver cross necklace is at the manor. I keep it in the drawer of my bedside table. I think about it every single day when I lie down to sleep, but I rarely look at it anymore. Knowing I'll never be able to touch the cool metal is a cross I'll have to forever bear.

I glance back at the witches. They're almost done with their ritual, so I'll soon be able to go home. Suddenly I ache to return to the manor and strip from my clothes, take a hot bath, and then slumber for a decade or two. I want to wash away the memories evoked by watching them tonight.

It's true I never wanted to be a vampire, but if Mamá were to see me now and ask how I am, I wouldn't deny that I'm starting to enjoy my new life. The daughter she remembers used to dream of marrying the love of her life and dying with him on the same day. But that girl died a long time ago. Now I'll never grow old, and I've accepted that eternal fate.

With their ritual complete, they walk in single file back to the house. A few witches linger behind to blow out the candles and carry in the relics. The sliding door shuts, and the remaining witches disappear behind the walls of a house I'll never again enter.

Mamá is in the kitchen window. She stares at the woods, and my pulse races. Can she see me? I blend into the night, but my crimson eyes pierce even the darkest shadows.

After another second, the outside light is turned off and Mamá is gone. I guess she didn't see me, watching, waiting, lurking in the shadows like the vampire I am.

I watch them from the forest behind my old house. They never know I'm here. If they did, they'd try to kill me. I know this to be true, yet I still patrol the woods.

I've been a vampire for an entire month, and that slow-passing time has helped me come to terms with something I've feared since the day I was forsaken: my coven won't accept me—not like this, not as a vampire. They will never take me back.

But I will protect them nonetheless.

ALSO BY DANIELLE ROSE

DARKHAVEN SAGA

Dark Secret

Dark Magic

Dark Promise

Dark Spell

Dark Curse

PIECES OF ME DUET

Lies We Keep

Truth We Bear

For a full list of Danielle's other titles,
visit her at DRoseAuthor.com

ACKNOWLEDGMENTS

I'm grateful for having so many inspiring and supportive people in my life.

To Heather, who is such an amazing person, a good friend, and someone who harnesses a level of creativity I aspire to obtain. You're such an integral part of my process. I look to you for guidance, support, and friendship, and I honestly feel as though I wouldn't be where I am today without your help. Never lose your shine.

I would also like to acknowledge my family, who offers unwavering support. I couldn't do this career without you. I love you all.

Shout out to the members of Petals & Thorns, my Facebook group. I adore you all so very much, and I hope my books bring you even an ounce of the joy you bring me. I can't imagine a better street team.

Finally, special thanks goes to the amazing team at Waterhouse Press. In the middle of writing this book, tragedy struck, and I lost my aunt. Her unexpected passing meant I wasn't able to meet my deadline. There's very little I fear more than disappointing my publisher, but their unwavering support sprouted a confidence in me I'll never shake.

Meredith, Jon, Jesse, Scott, Robyn, Haley, Jennifer, Yvonne, Amber, Keli Jo, Kurt, and the rest of the team behind making publishing not only possible but an actual *career* for me—*thank you*. From the bottom of my heart to the depths of my soul, your graciousness, love, and support helped me through darkness to embrace a light from which I've crafted this novel. I'm so very proud of this one, and I can't imagine a better home for it than Waterhouse Press.

ABOUT DANIELLE ROSE

Dubbed a "triple threat" by readers, Danielle Rose dabbles in many genres, including urban fantasy, suspense, and romance. The *USA Today* bestselling author holds a master of fine arts in creative writing from the University of Southern Maine.

Danielle is a self-professed sufferer of 'philes and an Oxford comma enthusiast. She prefers solitude to crowds, animals to people, four seasons to hellfire, nature to cities, and traveling as often as she breathes.

Visit her at DRoseAuthor.com